I0587370

A glorious cat and a rotten human mess

Travis scooted closer to Betty, and she touched his shoulder.

"You okay? Sounds like this came out of the blue."

"I'm maintaining for now. This stinks, but I don't know enough to know how to react. Except to wish he was here and could explain the whole mess. And that he'd moved here sooner so the two of you could have gotten to know each other. You would have loved him, and he..."

His voice caught, but before Betty could react, Pearla chirped and raised her head.

The cat arched into the caress before delicately making her way over to Travis's lap.

Because besides being gorgeous and glamorous, she apparently knew exactly what people needed, when they needed it.

Murder at the Fabulous Feline Emporium

Copyright © 2024 by Kari A. Kilgore

All rights reserved

Published 2024 by Spiral Publishing, Ltd.
www.SpiralPublishing.net

Book and cover design copyright © 2024 by Spiral Publishing, Ltd.

Cover art copyright © 2024 by design.isaeva@gmail.com | depositphotos.com

ISBN-13: 978-1-63992-030-3
Digital ISBN-13: 978-1-63992-034-1
Large Print ISBN-13: 978-1-63992-031-0

This book is licensed for your personal enjoyment only. All rights reserved. This is a work of fiction. All characters and events portrayed in this book are fictional, and any resemblance to real people or incidents is purely coincidental. This book, or parts thereof, may not be reproduced in any form without permission.

For everyone who helps care for our fabulous felines

MURDER AT THE FABULOUS FELINE EMPORIUM

KARI KILGORE

SPIRAL PUBLISHING, LTD.

CHAPTER 1

NOTHING WAS PRETTIER than Atlanta in the springtime, especially on the rare afternoons when traffic was light.

The gentle curves, broad lawns, and graceful old brick and stone houses along Ponce de Leon Avenue showed that off better than anywhere else in the city. The massive oak trees were still only green around the edges, late to put on their show as always. But the dogwoods already strutted their pink and white stuff, and rows of yellow and orange daffodils crowded forward demanding Betty's attention.

The sky was as blue as the robin eggs that would soon be appearing in nests all over her neighborhood, with only a few streaks of white clouds for contrast against the mid-morning sunshine.

A narrow park lay just to Betty's left as she slowed and stopped for a traffic light. A crowd of toddlers and their parents roamed slowly across the deep green grass, pastel baskets in hand. The only things more colorful than all the trees and flowers were those glorious Easter bonnets and dresses.

Betty turned down the classical station on the car's radio, then lowered the window on the passenger side. The glass slid down with barely a whisper. The squeals and giggles of children filled the air instead, along with the strong, rich scent of plants waking up.

Betty raised the window, smiling at the children, then frowning at the drift of yellowish dust floating across her windshield. Even with her allergy medicine, too many breaths full of Atlanta's bucketsful of pollen would deliver her to the cat groomer's shop in a state unfit for company.

And a strong gust of wind from a passing car might muss the holiday-appropriate curls she'd carefully arranged her short brown into despite the usual humid climate.

The risk of frizz and fuzz and general disruption was all too real.

Especially with a prime parental-judgement opportunity in her very near future.

The old-fashioned low granite curb glittered as Betty's white Volvo passed by, a reminder of her childhood that was disappearing everywhere else in the city. The rough, dull concrete the city kept using when the granite needed repair or replacement wouldn't be the same no matter what anyone said about easy maintenance.

Progress was good, of course, especially as the whole region continued its frantic preparation for the upcoming Olympic Games in the grand centennial year of 1996. But the insistence on sweeping away the past in an all-out sprint toward the future felt like a tragic mistake that would be impossible to undo once it was done.

She turned the radio back up just as the evocative strings of Copeland's lovely "Appalachian Spring" started playing. Well, they were a bit south of Appalachia here, but nothing could have been more perfect for such a glorious Southeastern Easter Sunday.

Betty adjusted the vent up toward her face so the air conditioning breathed across her skin. Spring might be beautiful here, but it was already getting hot enough for a most unladylike sweat, or worse, the onset of one of the wretched hot flashes she'd recently begun dealing with.

She hadn't expected such nonsense at barely forty-eight years old. But like her mother always said, the body's clock kept its own schedule, and all anyone could do was try to limit the damage.

Not that a bit of perspiration was actually *damage*, even when it struck without warning and for no good reason her logical mind could figure out.

Not in a city known for causing the most demure of

ladies and gentlemen to perspire long before summer really got rolling.

In fact, her Diet Coke was sweating in the cup holder right this minute. That would help cool her down every bit as well as the AC did, and it tasted a heck of a lot better. She wrinkled her nose at the tiny bubbles and the sharp smell of the dark soda, glad it hadn't gone flat.

That first cold drink chilled her mouth, throat, all the way down to her belly. Not quite as good as the icy glass bottles of her youth, but better than just about anything else you could drink while you were driving.

The bright red glow of the Krispy Kreme hot sign caught Betty's attention, and it nearly tempted her away from her errand and a lifetime of her mother Charlene's lectures about how she should do whatever it took to wrestle her curvy, comfortable figure into submission.

Far more importantly to Betty, her girlfriend Lee was quite fond of women with curves. And they quite happily took turns when it came to wrestling into submission.

Heat that had nothing to do with the weather or her unruly hormones rushed to her cheeks at that naughty thought. Surely not the sort of thing she should be contemplating on Easter Sunday, even if she hadn't been to church since she was sixteen.

Thinking about Lee wasn't doing herself any favors right now, either. Not with Lee off to visit her own lovely mother in Wisconsin for the whole damn week.

Betty'd honestly had a tough time turning down the invitation to join Lee and skip her own family obligation.

Anyway, if she were going to give in and enjoy herself (without Lee) rather than withholding such a simple pleasure, Krispy Kreme would be the way to do it. The big doughnut factory down on Ponce was legendary around here, especially for the late-night crowds who appreciated the opportunity to satisfy their cravings twenty-four hours a day. A perfectly fluffy and not-too-sweet doughnut barely cooled enough to hold the crisp/sticky/sweet icing was hard to resist no matter the time of day or night.

Betty glanced down at the waistline of her dark blue skirt and sighed.

Her light-blue blouse already pooched out a bit because that silly old skirt never had fit right, and she hadn't even been to the Easter luncheon with her family yet.

Maybe she should be good and save her appetite.

Or better yet, finally quit listening to childhood's scolding voices inside her head and stop worrying about an outdated outfit she hadn't even bought for herself and didn't much like anyway.

Enjoy every bite of what was sure to be a delicious meal with mostly wonderful company, especially now that the younger generation had banded together to keep their parental group's comments about weight and food and desserts to a minimum.

Then go home and change into clothing she actually looked and *felt* good in, and toss her current getup into the *Donate* box once and for all.

Then get together with like-minded friends for the real celebration, at least until Lee got home.

That sounded like a plan worth celebrating.

She exited her half-nervous, half-anticipatory musing just in time to realize the East Lake Feline Emporium was about a mile ahead on her right, so she needed to stake out her spot in that lane. Betty dared hope her good traffic luck would hold out all the way until she picked up their newly rescued best friend, fresh from an Easter makeover and ready to meet the family.

One of the many things she liked about the Emporium was their generous policy of offering services and pickups on holidays, so all their four-legged darlings could look their absolute best for the cat-approved festivities.

Hopefully sweet Pearla would be in a cheerful, friendly mood after her luxurious spa day, and not fierce and furious.

Much as Betty and Lee might wish they could predict their darling's moods and react accordingly, after only a couple of months, Pearla often kept her preferences and procedures mysterious and unexpected.

But wasn't that adventure and surprise one of the best things about sharing their lives and their hearts with a miniature white lion with stunning green eyes in the first place?

CHAPTER 2

BETTY TURNED INTO THE BROAD, scrupulously neat parking lot, absently wondering why no other cars were parked on the freshly surfaced blacktop. She expected the Emporium to be crowded this time of day as eager cat companions arrived to retrieve their newly clean and pampered friends, especially on a family-oriented holiday.

Right now, Betty had her choice of spots marked with white stencils of various stylized cat poses. She decided a fluffy beauty curled up for a nap would be her best bet, and maybe even influence Pearla's mood for the better.

The heat rising off that pretty surface embraced her like a wet electric blanket the second she stepped out of the car. She'd heard about Atlanta gradually turning into even *more* of a heat island with all the pavement, and the sweat popping out on her temples and just under her nose verified the dire prediction at once.

Perhaps that was why no one else was parked and waiting. A vehicle would transform into an oven after only a few minutes with heat radiating from both directions.

In her opinion, the Emporium's strict policy about never, ever leaving a cat or any other animal in a car made perfect sense. She believed the signs posted warning that windows would be broken if anyone was ever foolish enough to risk it.

She also understood why the owners of the tidy little white house converted into a feline oasis kept the sprawling magnolias surrounding the golf-course-quality lawn cut back from the parking lot. Beautiful as the trees were, they were notorious for dropping their big, shiny leaves everywhere, and the huge, wonderfully lemon-scented flowers had to go somewhere when their blooming time was done.

Onto vehicles or into them by way of their owner's shoes probably wasn't the best outcome for people willing to pay a small fortune to keep their furry friends extra clean and looking and smelling their best. Word was the sister business a couple of miles away—East Lake *Canine* Emporium, of course—was every bit as fastidious and well managed.

Still, Betty wished they'd planted something to keep their clients' cars from overheating quite so quickly.

She hurried along the pale sidewalk as quickly as she

dared in her sensible blue pumps, smiling at the multi-colored paw prints decorating the concrete.

A wide white awning overhead provided blessed relief from the solar assault.

The big windows flanking the house's soothing peach-colored door were mostly uncovered underneath the shade, featuring tasteful photos of cats in every possible contented pose around the edges.

Betty wouldn't have believed it until she saw it herself, but apparently people who were particularly nervous about leaving their companions tended to stand outside and watch the goings on in the comfy lobby for a long while before venturing in. The grooming and spoiling areas were in the back, so it wasn't like the poor worrywarts were going to see what really went on without a tour (which staff were happy to give).

But for some reason, observing people walking in and out with their favorite and often decorated carriers and seeing how the staff took notes and payments usually reassured them enough to finally go through the door and investigate.

With their cats safely at home, at least the first couple of visits.

Once Betty's dear friend Travis had recommended this fine establishment, she had no hesitation in trusting them to care for Pearla. She'd never known him to steer her wrong with any kind of advice, and the five gorgeous kitties he referred to as his Fabulous Feline Fleet were their own form of ringing endorsement.

Not only had the Fabulous Feline Fleet never been groomed anywhere else, but Travis had known Mr. Wilkenson, the owner of this fine establishment, since their college days.

She turned the brass doorknob shaped like a cat's face and sighed at the rush of cooler—and more importantly, drier—air inside. Not too cold for the precious warmth-loving creatures, and the bathing area was positively steamy. But Betty appreciated the consideration for her human, perimenopausal self.

The wonderful people she'd entrusted with her darling Pearla really did think of *every*thing.

The lobby's soft lavender and mint aromas washed over her before she closed the door behind her and let her eyes adjust to the relative dimness. After several seconds went by, she blinked, certain she was still not seeing clearly.

An empty parking lot was one thing, even during the normal pickup time.

But seeing what seemed like the entire building deserted, without lights or the sound of happy conversation? Not even the usual low relaxing music in the background?

Something was off here.

Betty glanced around again at the easy-clean but comfortable chairs with their cat-patterned cushions, silvery display shelves with all manner of treats, toys, and cozy beds, and a bookcase full of books covering all aspects of feline art, care, and fiction.

The section filled with cat-themed trinkets meant only for human enjoyment was a wonder to behold, and a first-rate temptation for emptying out her bank account.

The receptionist's desk was a sturdy white model that held a computer disguised by a video screen showing cats of all shapes and sizes playing.

Closed doors on either side of the desk led to the heart of the business, with carefully designed tubs, drying cages, and several luxurious waiting areas for cats fancied up and ready to go home.

But Betty didn't hear a thing besides her shoes tapping on the sky-blue tile under her feet.

She didn't need to glance at her watch to make sure she had the time right, and she wasn't likely to mix up an ordinary day with Easter Sunday.

The first uneasy stirrings of worry twisted through her belly.

Where in the world was everyone?

And where was *Pearla*?

They'd barely started getting to know each other, and Betty and Lee had been working hard to make sure Pearla felt safe and secure after her previous life as a stray and weeks spent in the shelter.

She raised one hand, meaning to push the door to the back open, then hesitated.

If something dreadful had happened, maybe she shouldn't charge right in.

But the thought of that something dreadful

happening to her cat gave her enough courage to at least knock on the door.

She'd figure out the rest when the time came.

"Hello? Is anyone here?" she called.

Something shuffled on the other side of the door, and quick footsteps moved toward her.

Too light and quick to be an assailant, right?

And surely someone intending to cause her harm would make more of an effort to be quiet.

Wouldn't they?

CHAPTER 3

Betty didn't realize her hand was still at knocking height until the door opened and a young woman drew back with an expression of alarm.

Her black hair was pulled into a neat ponytail, and she wore the emporium's uniform of a peach golf shirt with a stylized logo of three snuggling cats embroidered in metallic gold thread on one side. The usual brightly colorful nametag was missing from the other side.

Her brown eyes were wide and frightened, and she held one hand over her mouth.

"I'm sorry, I didn't mean to scare you." Betty clenched her own hands at her waist. "I'm here to pick up Pearla Compton?"

The woman frowned as she lowered her hand, now looking confused, before she closed her eyes for a second and sighed.

"Oh dear, you have nothing to apologize for, Ms.

Compton. I thought I'd called everyone to let them know what's going on. I obviously forgot to lock the door."

The woman hurried across the empty lobby and did just that before turning back to Betty.

"I truly am sorry, Ms. Compton. I'd hoped everyone either had a cell phone or checked their messages. Pearla's just fine."

A wave of departing tension left Betty nearly swooning.

Unfortunately it also triggered one of her internal furnace episodes, leaving her chest, face, and arms feeling like the sun blazed from under her skin. Hopefully she could escape before it got worse and left her uncomfortably damp with no way to hide it.

"No cell phone for me, and I wouldn't use one while I was driving. Those things are dangerous. Please, call me Betty. In any case, if you could take me to Pearla so we can get out of your way, I'd greatly appreciate it. Her carrier is here as well."

The woman blinked, then shook her head.

"I'm afraid I can't take you back, but if you give me a few minutes, I can bring her up front. And I just realized I never introduced myself. We've just been so distressed with everything that's... Anyway, I'm Cortney Martinez. I should have a name tag, but I only started last week."

Betty nodded and held out her hand. Cortney's was dry and kind of rough, like she spent her hours here doing baths or blow drying instead of working in the lobby. That might help explain her distress.

"Pleased to meet you, Cortney. We've only had Pearla for a couple of months, and I've had the tour already. So I'd love to go back with you and get her if I can. I want to make sure she sees a familiar face as soon as possible after her first time here. And I'm terribly sorry to rush you, but we have a party we need to get to."

Cortney wrung her hands, looking for all the world like she hoped a grownup would swoop in and save her. The roughened skin made a soft, hissing noise.

Now that she knew Pearla was okay, Betty's curiosity jumped even higher.

"Well, this is the problem," Cortney said, her hands still wrestling each other. "I've never checked one of the cats out before. You would have seen Dave when you dropped Pearla off this morning, but he left for the day because only a couple of cats are left. See, I normally work in the back. The only reason I'm here is to keep an eye on things until the people from the shelter arrive to take the cats who haven't gone home yet."

"*What?*" Betty drew herself up, aware she was nearly shouting but unable to stop herself. "Pearla will absolutely *not* be going to a shelter. I'm standing right here, and she already spent more than enough time without a home. I'm perfectly capable of getting her myself. Then if you don't know how to settle things, I can pay the bill with Mr. Wilkenson tomorrow. Hopefully things will be back to normal by then."

Cortney held up both hands, and Betty was alarmed to see how badly she was shaking.

"Oh no, I'm only making things worse. They're not *keeping* the cats, we'd never let that happen. It's just that we don't have the facilities to keep them overnight, and we had to close so suddenly. I was going to... Well, I was going to call Dave to ask for help with getting Pearla ready to go home."

Betty crossed her arms, trying to ignore how sweaty they were.

"I think we need to back up for a minute. What exactly has happened here? I may not have been a client here until today, but I *have* lived in the neighborhood my whole life. My best friend knows the owner and can get in touch, or maybe I can find someone else to help."

Cortney looked at the floor long enough that Betty opened her mouth to repeat her words.

But the tears standing in the young woman's eyes when she looked back up froze the words in Betty's throat.

"That's just the problem, Ms.... Betty. Mr. Wilkenson, he's dead. I found him when I stopped by his office to see if he wanted to order lunch with us. That's the *real* reason I'm here by myself. I hated to call the shelter, but I didn't know what else to do. Dave went to talk to the police, that's why he left early. Everyone else is on vacation."

She hitched in a couple of breaths and her hands returned to their whispery gyrations.

"I'm *so* sorry to cause you and Pearla all this trouble."

All of Betty's frustration and worry dissolved when Cortney's head slumped forward and she started crying. She reached out and touched one of those endlessly twisting hands.

Cortney immediately stepped forward into Betty's hastily outstretched arms, sobbing like an exhausted child. Which of course snapped Betty into her much-loved and reassuringly familiar role as a comforting auntie.

She was nothing but grateful to do something that made sense on a day that had turned out to be anything but ordinary.

"There there, it's all going to be okay." She patted and rubbed Cortney's shoulders. "Things like this are awful when you're all by yourself. I'll help you figure out what to do."

CHAPTER 4

AFTER A FEW MINUTES that had Betty needing to wipe her own eyes, Cortney finally took a huge breath and stepped back. The poor girl's face was bright red, and she rushed over to the receptionist's desk to fetch several tissues. She handed some to Betty and used the rest on her own cheeks.

Once her words got started, they picked up speed like a snowball rolling downhill.

"I'm sorry, again, for falling apart like that. It's just... I wasn't prepared for this at all when I walked into Mr. Wilkenson's, you know? And he was slumped over at his desk, almost like he was asleep. He does that sometimes, takes a nap around lunchtime. Well, he *did* do that. But he didn't move even when I knocked on the door or pushed on his shoulder. I freaked out more than I should have. I think I scared Dave half to death, and all the poor cats."

Now she was wringing the tissues into bits of snow falling onto the tile.

"Let's back up again," Betty said. She did just that, stepping backward until she could sit on one of the cat-cushion chairs. Thankfully Cortney did the same, still holding on to the remnants of her tissue. "Are the cats okay? Do they need water or anything?"

Cortney stared at her wide-eyed.

"I didn't mean anything that bad by calling the shelter, they're fine right now. They have water and their tiny litterboxes. I just checked on Pearla before you came in. She was curled up sound asleep." She paused for a breath and glanced up at Betty, her smile shy.

"I groomed her this morning. And it was my absolute pleasure. She's silky and gorgeous and *so* well-behaved."

Betty couldn't stop her proud smile.

"I'm so glad to hear that. She's usually a sweetheart at home, but you never know with a different place and new people."

"And *water* with cats. I always make sure to keep it and the shampoo nice and warm and put the shower curtain behind me so they'll stay calm, but some of them won't have it no matter how nice I try to keep things." She glanced around as if someone might have sneaked into the lobby.

"Listen, since you're here and she's such a good kitty, I can go ahead and bring her out. I don't know who's going to handle the billing now that...from now on, but I don't want to keep you apart."

Betty considered, trying to weigh her wish to see Pearla against her increasing desire to not be late for the party against Cortney's obvious distress.

Worry about Cortney stuck here alone—and not wanting any cat to go to the shelter, even for a few hours—won out.

"How about this?" Betty said. "Sounds like she'll be fine for a little while longer. I'll call my friend Travis, the one who went to college with Mr. Wilkenson. He's here all the time with his five cats, so I suspect he'll be willing to come over and help. He'll need to know what happened, and I'd rather he heard it from me instead of somewhere else. I'd say between the three of us, we can figure out somewhere else to keep any other cats still here instead of taking them to the shelter."

Relief so clear it was almost funny washed across Cortney's face before she composed herself.

"Didn't you say you had a party to get to? I know it's Easter Sunday and all."

"I think my family will understand if I'm a little late. This will sound like another reason to get a cell phone, which Travis has been trying to talk me into for a while now, but can I use your phone, please?"

"Of course!" Cortney jumped up and dashed halfway to the desk before she turned back, one hand on her chest. "Are you *sure* you don't mind? It has been a little creepy staying here alone after what happened, but I don't want to interrupt all your plans."

Betty got to her feet, shaking her head.

"As long as I eventually bring Pearla by for everyone to meet, they'll be perfectly fine as long as I let them know. It's not like we don't get together all the time anyway."

Cortney clasped both hands above her heart and smiled.

"Thank you so much. You make any calls you need to, I'll try the other clients again, then I'll go get your sweet kitty."

CHAPTER 5

LESS THAN AN HOUR LATER, Betty sat in the same lobby, far more comfortable than she'd been when she walked in.

Travis had quickly agreed not only to drop by the Emporium, but he'd also brought along a pair of cool brown shorts and a green t-shirt for her to change into. She certainly never would have imagined sitting on the floor, cross-legged and perched on one of the thickest cat beds in stock, if she still had her mother-approved skirt on.

He'd changed from what he called his marriage-induced getup, trading in an afternoon dressed for his wife Nina's golf-mad in-laws without hesitation. Betty wasn't surprised to hear Nina had sent him with her sympathy and only a tinge of jealousy that she couldn't manage to wrangle herself out of the obligation.

The resulting denim shorts, faded Atlanta Braves t-shirt, and rumpled brown hair suited him a lot better. His red and swollen eyes and generally heartbroken demeanor did not.

Betty hated the way he restrained his upset at losing his friend when he'd usually talk to her about it, but she admired the way he held off on his usual thousand-and-one questions, giving Cortney a chance to relax.

She expected to hear a lot more from him about all of this before too much more time passed. Listening was the least she could do after years spent crying on each other's shoulders almost as much as they'd laughed and celebrated together.

The remaining clients stopping by to pick up their cats—with a great deal of sympathy and understanding —put Cortney even more at ease.

Pearla, on the other hand, had raced around the lobby for several minutes as soon as Cortney brought her out, sniffing every corner, prancing and chirping as if she knew exactly how stunning her flouncing white coat looked. She paused long enough in the midst of basking in her much-deserved admiration to accept their offerings of a bit of food and water.

Then, satisfied that everyone had seen how beautiful she was, she curled up in Betty's lap and fell sound asleep.

The fresh, proper New York-style bagels, cream cheese, and coffee Travis supplied served as a fine stand-in for the Easter brunch Betty was missing. Thankfully Betty'd gotten Katie—her upset but understanding sister—when she called rather than either of her fussy and easily scandalized parents.

The best part was the way Cortney eventually managed to settle herself on one of the cat beds to join in the feast. Her anxious fidgeting decreased steadily until all Betty caught was an occasional twirl of her ponytail.

"Thank you for stopping by, Travis," Cortney said as she crumpled the wrapper on the bagel she'd demolished in record time. "We were just about to order lunch when everything went wrong."

"You are quite welcome." He glanced at Betty, and she nodded. His eyes turned redder but his face and voice stayed calm. "Listen, I know you're still upset, and I understand why. But I have to ask about what happened to Joey. I pretty much grew up with the guy. I hadn't heard a word until Betty called."

Cortney stared at him, and Betty was afraid she'd start crying again. But Cortney only took a couple of deep breaths before answering.

"I really appreciate you coming over here, since you knew him and all. And I'm *so* sorry you lost your friend. I can't tell you too much because I don't know much. Like I told Betty, I thought he was asleep. The police showed up with the coroner and had a good look around, and they asked us to keep Mr. Wilkenson's office locked up in case they find anything with their tests and all. But otherwise, they didn't say anything about finding evidence or anything like that. Not that they wanted to tell me about, anyway."

Travis shook his head, and Betty caught his jaw clenching a couple of times.

"I just don't understand it. Joey was always healthy as a horse. Or a cat, I guess I should say. Took great care of himself, ate right. About the only bad habit he had was drinking coffee pretty much 24/7. Are you sure the police didn't say *anything* else?"

"Nothing that I heard them talk about." Cortney's chin trembled for a second, but she held it together. "They weren't in a rush or calling in backup. They took a bunch of pictures and I think they checked for fingerprints and stuff like that."

"Have you heard anything from Dave?" Betty said. "Didn't he go talk to the police?"

Cortney frowned. "Not yet. I'm pretty sure he was going with them to go talk to Mr. Wilkenson's wife. But he probably thinks I already closed up and went home. I can try to call him if you want."

Travis rubbed his forehead.

"I guess that can wait. I should stop by and talk to Joey's wife too. Hell, I'll probably hear from the police at some point, but I doubt I can help them. Far as I know, pretty much everyone else liked Joey as much as I did."

"So you think they'll find something," Betty said. "In his bloodwork or whatever they're doing. Otherwise why would they need to talk to you?"

At Cortney's sharp breath, Betty regretted the question. But she still wanted to know.

Travis shrugged and tried to smile, and she doubted he fooled Cortney, either.

"That's the only thing that makes sense to me. We always joked about getting older, you know? How we were about to turn into creaky old men and we could lean on each other's shoulders. But we talked about our health stuff at the same time. Unless he was keeping something from me and doing a great acting job, he was fine."

Cortney got to her feet a lot faster than either Betty or Travis could have managed.

"I'm going to go ahead and call Dave. He might be home by now unless things went really bad with the police. And you've got me wondering what might have happened now."

Before anyone else could say a word, she was at the desk with the phone in her hand.

Travis scooted closer to Betty, and she touched his shoulder.

"You okay? Sounds like this came out of the blue."

He sighed and glanced at Cortney, who was still on the phone. When he looked back, his eyes were redder than ever.

"I'm maintaining for now. This stinks, but I don't know enough to know how to react. Except to wish he was here and could explain the whole mess. And that he'd moved here sooner so the two of you could have gotten to know each other. You would have loved him, and he..."

His voice caught, but before Betty could react, Pearla chirped and raised her head, blinking at whatever had interrupted her royal slumber. Then she stood and stretched her legs one at a time, digging her claws into Betty's bare legs.

"Thank goodness for freshly trimmed nails," she said, rubbing her hand along Pearla's back, glad for the distraction for Travis and for herself. The cat arched into the caress before delicately making her way over to Travis's lap.

Because besides being gorgeous and glamorous, she apparently knew exactly what people needed, when they needed it.

"Well aren't you a confident little thing?" He waited until she shook her hair back out to maximum fluffiness and rearranged herself for another nap before petting her. "I knew she'd find a good home with you two."

"So far so good, but she hasn't met my parents yet."

They watched Cortney hang up and stare into space for several seconds before she walked toward them.

"Nothing so far, but the police said some of the tests can take a while. We're still supposed to keep the office locked, and they might want to talk to some of us. To tell you the truth, it sounds to me like they're surprised about what happened, too."

"I'd be upset if they weren't." Travis shot a warning

glance Betty's way. "Can we help you close up, Cortney? That way we can all get to what's left of the day."

Cortney blinked and looked around, as if a huge mess of cat hair might have exploded in the lobby over the last few minutes.

"There's not much to do, but thank you. I just have to lock everything up and head out. I know you two didn't have to stay, but it really helped me get my head clear."

Betty got up, using one of the cat cushion chairs for balance and not caring who noticed. Travis took his time shifting Pearla onto the bed by herself before he stood.

Pearla purred without opening her eyes.

"I figure it was the least we could do," Betty said, "to thank you for taking such good care of our kitties. Pearla looks wonderful, and Travis always raves about how his bunch turn out."

"Let me just check the back to make sure."

Cortney went through one of the closed doors, and Betty was glad to see she had a little spring in her step.

She was surprised when Travis grabbed her arm.

CHAPTER 6

"Listen," Travis said, his voice low and rough, "I didn't want to say anything while she was in here, but I really want to get a look at that office. I've known Joey for a long damn time, and I'm telling you something doesn't make sense here."

"Sounds like they're doing toxicology tests and I'd guess an autopsy. You think they're still going to miss something?"

He shook his head slowly. "I don't know what they'll find or what they won't. But I knew him better than this poor kid did, and probably better than anyone in the police department did. Dave's another sweet kid who's been here longer, but that's hardly the same. I suppose someone could have gotten him at home, sure. I doubt it, though. Too many ways to get caught."

Betty glanced toward the closed door.

"What, you want to just charge back there? She's

jumpy enough that she might go right through the roof. And she said the office is locked."

Travis smiled, but it was nowhere near his usual bright and open expression. This was cold and closed off.

"Don't worry about the door. There's a trick to it. I'm just going to walk back there and see what happens. Maybe you can ask her to help getting Pearla into her carrier."

Crazy as it sounded, Betty knew she wasn't going to talk him out of it. She'd known him too long to miss that stubborn and determined look in his eyes.

And maybe he had a point. She'd never known him to be impulsive or paranoid.

"All right," she said, poking his chest. "But you be quick. I don't want to upset Cortney again on top of everything else that's happened today."

"I don't need long." Travis started toward the door, then turned back. "I owe you, Betty."

She sighed, checked to make sure Pearla was still asleep, then followed Travis.

"You sure do, buddy," she said under her breath. "Don't think I'm going to forget that."

The door swung in before Travis could open it, and Cortney drew back.

"Is something wrong?" she said, one hand on her chest. "Did Dave call back, or the police?"

"Not yet," Travis said. "I hate to ask, but can I use the restroom? I'll only be a minute."

Cortney's eyebrows drew together for a second before she answered.

"I guess so. I'm sure you know where it is?"

"I do. Thanks."

He went in without looking at Betty. Before she could say anything, Cortney frowned.

"I'd better clean all of this up. I guess it would be hard to explain why all the beds are on the floor first thing in the morning, or why there are bagel crumbs I'm sure I missed. Assuming we're open tomorrow at all."

Betty was surprised by a bolt of preemptive unhappiness. It hadn't really occurred to her that the Emporium might not last after the owner was gone. She'd been too focused on calming Cortney down and retrieving her own sweet kitty.

The idea of having to find somewhere else she trusted to take care of Pearla made her feel more tired than she wanted to admit. And of course everyone who worked here would suffer a whole lot more.

"It will go pretty quick if we both do it," she said. "Then maybe you can help me get Pearla back into her carrier. She goes in pretty well the first time, but she doesn't care for getting back in once she's free."

Cortney rolled her eyes and smiled fondly at the beautiful white cat.

"She didn't like it one bit when I finished grooming her. Probably because she'd never met me before. Sure, I'll help."

Only a few minutes later, they had the beds brushed off and back on the shelves, all the stray bagel bits swept up, and Pearla safely tucked into her carrier with remarkably little fuss. Cortney assured Betty that the gorgeous girl had utilized her tiny litterbox recently enough to handle the drive.

Betty was starting to get nervous about Travis taking so long when he quietly walked out, closing the door behind him. When he met her curious gaze, he nodded the tiniest bit before picking up the carrier.

She had to admit the pale-blue crate Lee had decorated with photos of Pearla looked kind of silly in his big hand, but she didn't feel the least bit like laughing.

"That should be everything," Cortney said. "Thank you both again for keeping me company. Want me to let you know if I hear anything else?"

"I'd appreciate it," Betty said before Travis had a chance to give detailed instructions. "You've got both our numbers, but you can just call one of us. We'll pass the information along to each other."

They walked out into the parking lot, and Betty wasn't especially happy with how much hotter it had gotten while they were inside. Atlanta had once again proven how brutal even the early spring could be.

Sweat covered her face and arms in seconds, and she was afraid Travis would want to stand right there in the broiling parking lot to discuss whatever he'd found.

He surprised her by going to her car and waiting

instead of getting into his little blue Prius parked right beside her Volvo.

Then Cortney surprised her even more by holding her arms out for a hug.

"I couldn't have gotten through the day without you," she said. "Now get your sweet kitty home and out of this heat."

"Will do. Go take care of yourself, Cortney. Get some rest."

Without asking what Travis wanted to do, Betty rolled all the windows down to let the overcooked air billow out, hot enough to make the emporium and glossy magnolia leaves look wavy. Only then did she get in long enough to start her car and get the air conditioner going on high. For her own sake as much as Pearla's.

They waved as Cortney drove by in a silver sedan that was well kept, but obviously about as old as she was.

Travis waited until the car was out of sight before speaking.

"I *knew* there was a problem," he said, handing the carrier to Betty. "Let's get in so I don't melt onto the pavement."

"Welcome to my life, even when it's cold outside. Come on."

CHAPTER 7

PEARLA quite reasonably fussed at being buckled into the back seat rather than the front. A creature so lovely and adorable should never be out of sight of anyone who might happen to pass by and glance inside.

That task accomplished—and Pearla's complaints down to an occasional yowl—Betty slid into the driver's seat with a relieved sigh as the cold air blasted her. She'd keep sweating for a while, sure. But at least the waterworks should finally get the hint that it was time to decrease their output.

"Spill it, Travis. I assume you managed to break into the office despite police orders not to?"

He snorted. "It's not hard, not even a little bit. Joey showed me as soon as the place opened. He never kept anything all that valuable in there because the door was hung crooked, or the jam was set wrong, something.

Anyway, all it takes is lifting the knob the right way and a good shove. Don't worry, I didn't touch anything."

"But did you *find* anything."

He drummed his fingers on the door.

"It's what I *didn't* find. I've never seen Joey at any job he's ever had without his silly Windy City coffee mug. Hell, he had it with him most of the time as far as I could tell, but he took it to work every single day. Has since 1985 or so."

Betty blinked, not sure how to respond to such an unexpected response.

"Maybe it got broken?"

Travis shook his head.

"Not likely. It was metal. I've got one just like it at home, and that thing has been through the wars. A little scratched and dented, but perfectly usable. Joey *loved* that thing. We went on a road trip to Chicago over spring break right before we graduated from college. Us and a couple of other guys."

He laughed softly, and Betty wondered if he knew he was crying.

"Bunch of dumb kids in an old station wagon of all things. I can't even remember why we picked Chicago. Anyway, we were young and stupid enough to eat at Taco Bell for most of the trip. You know, it was open late and what we could afford. Four guys that age, lots of bean burritos, in the car for hours. You can imagine the rest."

"I can. I grew up with a herd of boy cousins, and

they didn't even need the beans. To tell you the truth, us girl cousins were probably worse. So naturally you all got Windy City mugs for your windy road trip, huh? And now Joey's is missing."

Travis looked at her, and her heart broke at the misery in his face.

"It's missing. I know it sounds like I'm grasping, and maybe I am. But if it's not at his house or in his car, I'm telling you there's a good reason for that."

Betty turned in her seat, trying to see the small employees parking lot around to the side.

"Is his car here? I never thought to ask Cortney about that."

"I walked back there to check before I came in with the bagels. It's not here, but he usually walks to work, even in the heat. I can ask his wife if he did this morning, and I will. If it's not back at his house, there's another lead someone needs to chase down."

Travis held his breath and stared straight ahead for several seconds, as if he had a sudden intense interest in the row of azaleas at the edge of the Emporium's yard, currently blooming in red, pink, and white. When he breathed out, it was hard enough to fog the windshield.

"I'm sure I sound like a lunatic or some kind of warped conspiracy theory nut. Right this minute I kind of feel that way. I know people get blindsided by things like this every single day, when someone they thought was healthy suddenly drops dead. But something's not right here, Betty. I feel that in my bones."

He rolled his head from one shoulder to the other, then dropped his chin down toward his chest. By the time he looked at Betty, his eyes were hard but no longer red.

"Okay," she said. "I wasn't lucky enough to meet you back when Joey did, though I think I was pretty damn lucky to miss that particular road trip. But you've been a hell of a good friend to me for a long time. I wish I'd gotten to know him. I'll help you any way I can to figure out what happened."

He stared long enough that she thought he was going to refuse, or maybe really fall apart.

Instead he leaned over for a quick hug.

"I wish you'd had a chance to get to know him, too. I guess I figured since he finally moved down here and you just started bringing your precious girl here, it was just a matter of time until we all got together. Time he didn't have, as it turns out. He was almost as good as you are at passing for a typical, straight-laced good citizen, while secretly being as wicked and strange as me."

Pearla let out an especially plaintive—and loud—*yowl* then, and Travis scrubbed his face with both hands.

"I've kept you two long enough. Better get princess home and let her get settled with her new hairdo. When does Lee get back?"

"Not until next week, which is way longer than I'd like. I'd love to go home, even without her there, but I guess we should head over for the tail end of the big family gathering. I've already been hearing complaints about missing St. Patrick's Day."

Travis rolled his eyes and grinned, almost a normal one.

"And I thought I had it bad with my in-laws insisting on dragging us out to their uptight and precious golf club three or four times a year. I'd offer to join you for moral support, but that would only give your folks more material to sharpen and use as verbal spears. They're not exactly members of my fan club and never have been. The Comptons really do scan the calendar for every excuse for a guilt trip, don't they?"

"They do. Invented a few of their own while they were at it. You know *I'm* a member of your fan club if that helps. You going to be all right?"

He closed his eyes and shrugged.

"It does help. I think I'll be okay. Today's the easy part. It's going to get worse over time, between me wanting to pick up the phone and call him and however long it takes me to stop doing that because I finally realize he's gone. That day will probably be the worst. I'll let you know if I find out anything."

"I'll do the same."

She waited for him to get out and made sure his car started before she backed out. Pearla let out another lamenting cry when the car started moving.

"I understand, sweetheart. I'd rather go home, too. But maybe they'll have some kind of good kitty welcome-to-the-family gift for you."

CHAPTER 8

BETTY DID her best to get back into her determined-to-stay-calm family-friendly mode on the drive over. But the effort was probably doomed to failure since she refused to get back into her uncomfortable and very-much-not-*her* skirt and blouse.

Maybe because of that, or simply because the delay meant she ended up hitting the combined after-brunch and pre-barbeque rush, her commute ended up a pure misery.

She managed to get stopped by every red light, held up in every one of Atlanta's endless mystery traffic snarls, and even stuck behind a couple of wrecks with no obvious cause besides the stress and bad mood of a day full of enforced family togetherness.

Pearla added her own special chorus of frustrated yowls that were a perfect match to Betty's favorite nerve-soothing classical station switching to their news hour.

By the time her expected twenty minutes stretched into *over* an hour, she'd long since switched to a classic rock station, but not nearly loud enough to calm her down.

The tension-and-heat-induced hot flashes only added to her disheveled appearance, leaving her hair in exactly the steam-fuzzed mess she'd set out to avoid that morning.

So of course she finally arrived at her sister Katie's oh-so-perfect suburban paradise in no mood or shape for company.

The sprawling two-story pale blue confection couldn't be called large for the neighborhood, not with far larger and showier McMansions crammed into their lots in close proximity. But Betty was pretty sure the cozy Craftsman bungalow she shared with Lee and Pearla would fit inside twice over with a little room to spare.

Betty knew one reason Katie and her husband had grabbed it was the location at the end of the curving, house-packed road, giving them a good bit more privacy and space for a kid- and gardener-friendly yard. They'd taken full advantage in the seven years since they moved in.

A neat row of flower beds along the edges of the front yard were a riot of color that changed with the seasons, and today they spilled over with tulips in every shade of the rainbow.

The flat expanse in the middle did have the

required mass of deep green grass, which was currently decorated with a cheery display of huge carboard Easter eggs, baskets, and bright-eyed Easter bunnies, much like the tiny lawns in the rest of the neighborhood.

Betty's favorite—and a sure sign that her stealth oddball sister hadn't fully succumbed to her suburban lifestyle—was a decidedly creepy stuffed bunny peeking over the tall wooden fence surrounding the back yard. Besides standing a good nine feet tall, the somewhat manic rabbit had red eyes open too wide to be comforting to go with rather prominent teeth.

Even better was the way their parents had complained about the creepy cottontail when Betty brought it home a few years ago, wondering what on *earth* the neighbors might think.

Betty, Katie, and a few of their similarly inappropriate cousins and their partners had offered the unusual decoration a giggly toast late that Sunday night.

The alarming number of cars still crowding the driveway and along the street made it clear she wasn't as late as she might have wished after an already stressful day.

But the pastel-flower-festooned front door opened before she could contemplate driving away rather than wedging her Volvo into the last available space before crossing into neighbor territory.

Katie stepped out onto the stoop, a springtime vision in an intense pink sundress with a wide black belt, with her curly brown hair as carefully arranged as Betty's had been a couple of hours ago.

A vision who waved one arm in the air, then pointed firmly at the stoop. An unmistakable sisterly suggestion that Betty get her backside into the house.

Now.

Or else.

And Katie—probably due just as much to her majorly successful career as an attorney as to her sisterly experience—knew how to make that *or else* count like no one else.

Betty shook her head, but pulled forward into the barely-big-enough spot at the same time.

"Okay sweet Pearla, we're here. I'm sorry it took so long, but your Auntie Katie promised she'd have food, water, and a litterbox ready for you. She even tucked her own kitties away into their sunroom paradise for your visit so you can explore."

Pearla replied with a low growl entirely unlike her heart-wrenching yowls.

Fairly new cat person or not, Betty understood the cat-equivalent of Katie's *or else* when she heard it.

A quick glance in the mirror made it clear her hair was more hopeless than her mood, so she grabbed one of the elastic bands she kept in her glovebox in case of this sort of emergency. A messy, last-minute ponytail might not exactly look pulled together, but getting her heavy hair off her neck was worth the likely parental sniffs of disappointment.

This time the air felt like opening the dishwasher drawer too soon after the cycle completed. Nowhere near the August levels of misery that were coming, but hardly conducive to comfortable time spent in the back-yard, even if she didn't have judgement for all her wardrobe and presentation sins to look forward to.

"Come on, poor baby. At least one of us will get petted and fussed over after a tough day."

Instead of holding the crate by the handle, Betty held it against her chest, only a little bit like a shield. She pretended to herself that with all nine pounds of Pearla shifting around inside she needed the better grip to keep from dropping it.

Katie glanced behind her before closing the door and hurrying across the yard, bare feet with perfectly pink toenails sinking into the thick mat of weed-free grass.

"I'm sure you have a great reason why you're so late. Here, let me take my kitty niece so you can greet the parents without such adorable little armor to hide behind. What are you *wearing*?"

"Good to see you too, Katie." Betty handed the crate over, relieved and grateful when Pearla turned on the charm with a series of sweet chirrups.

Katie was solidly on her side and always had been, but cute-critter distraction in a weird situation was always a good thing.

"Oh you are just *gorgeous*, aren't you? No, I don't mean you, Betty, you look... Well, you look like your normal self, which wasn't the plan today at all. You'll have to tell me what's going on with poor Travis, but not until after we get this party over with and everyone out of here. I doubt the parental units have changed their truly unreasonable opinions about him."

Betty followed, out of excuses to avoid entering the family fray, and unwilling to get into their parents' long-standing dislike of one of her best friends.

"Why do you have these big bashes if you dislike them so much?"

Katie stopped in front of the door, scowling at if Betty had just said she hoped she wasn't too late for the game where the whole family would strip naked, cover themselves in honey, and roll around in a giant fire ant nest in the front yard.

"I absolutely love having big bashes with people who actually appreciate them and show up to have fun instead of making spreadsheets of everything I could have done better. *You* know that since *you're* always on the guest list. The only reason I host for the obligatory family holidays is so I can get my ass to the cocktails quicker when it's all over. If I had to drive home first, I'd probably have to pull over for a screaming fit and scare the kids. Now get *your* ass inside before they come out looking for us!"

Betty couldn't argue with any of that, since Katie did throw the best parties of anyone she knew. Especially the parties geared more for grownups who weren't their parents or their similarly uptight friends, of course.

Even before the bizarre turn her day had taken, this wasn't going to be one of those fun, laid back, relaxing events.

Now the best she could hope for was getting it over with.

CHAPTER 9

THE MASSIVE PAPER bouquet of spring flowers on the front door was a fine introduction to the explosion of pastel inside. Katie had brought out piles of spring-colored pillows, throw rugs and blankets, and vases full of fresh blossoms perched on every available surface. Bowls that had probably been heaped full of every Easter-themed candy ever produced covered the huge coffee table, well picked over by adult and child alike.

Betty was pleasantly surprised to only see a handful of adults relaxing on Katie's comfortable sofas and chairs, all of them around her age.

Katie leaned close enough to speak for Betty's ears only.

"Don't worry, all the real grownups are out back with the maniac kids, and all the mean aunts and uncles have already fled the scene. Our charming-as-always parents will get to you soon enough." Then she held up

Pearla's carrier. "Look who's here! The guest of honor and her casual-Friday escort!"

Cat-companions all, everyone offered quiet worship while Pearla first explored the room, sniffing the trails of the cats she wouldn't be meeting today, then paid a discrete visit to the litterbox stashed behind a huge cardboard cutout of a friendly looking Easter bunny.

Properly refreshed, she finally started her rounds of receiving appropriate adoration.

Betty did her best to stay out of the way so she could catch her breath, and give her kitty a chance to get over being mad. But only a couple of minutes went by before someone tapped her shoulder.

She turned to see her cousin Stacie, another of the childfree renegades of the family. She'd toed the line when it came to clothing, choosing a sedate and cheery lavender pantsuit with a pale green blouse underneath.

But she spoke her own language by dyeing her spiky short hair and coordinating her assorted ear piercings to match.

"Glad to see another hooligan made it." She handed Betty a tulip-shaped glass that fizzed like a mimosa with barely enough orange juice to provide the color. "We need reinforcements against the regulators out back. They did notice your absence, and used it against all the rest of us."

"Sorry about that. They'll get around to me soon enough, I promise. It's been a hell of a day."

Stacie held up her own tulip and Betty tapped it.

"To continuing to confound the previous generation," Stacie said.

"Long may we endure."

The mimosa was indeed barely disguised champagne, and the dry undercurrent to the sweet orange juice was exactly what Betty needed.

"Sure this is safe to drink on such a hot day?" Betty said. "I swear I can feel my liver contracting."

Stacie winked and sipped her own drink.

"If you can't trust the toxicologist of the family, who can you trust? I might suggest taking in some electrolytes if you're going to have more than a couple, but that's up to you. The peanut and pretzel snack mix should do nicely. Was Katie telling the truth about you finding a dead body?"

"Not this time. The body was gone by the time I arrived."

Stacie listened to the whole sorry tale with her usual intense concentration. Betty knew she'd be able to repeat the whole thing pretty much word for word no matter how many cocktails went down.

"Do you think your friend is overreacting? About the death being suspicious?"

Betty watched Pearla jump onto a sofa between two of her younger cousins and await the required adoration.

"I think he's upset, but he knew the poor guy for decades. I never got the chance to meet him. I'm not sure if it was murder, no. But I *am* sure if Travis smells something off, there's some kind of reason to believe him."

Stacie nodded, tapping a fingernail that matched her green blouse against the glass.

"Well, I can't say a word officially or speak for the lab. But if you happen to need something analyzed, you know where to find me. And right now, I'm going to find a different corner to lurk in. Good luck."

She sauntered across the room, which had gotten a lot more quiet and much less relaxing.

Betty didn't have to turn to know what had changed.

The parents had entered the party.

Sure enough, her father's voice cut across the now-quiet conversation.

"I'm quite relieved to see you made it, Betty. We were starting to wonder if you'd manage to put in an appearance this time or if you'd gotten distracted."

Mr. Walter Edward Compton wasn't dressed for the golf club like Travis's in-laws by any means. But no one would ever mistake his clothing for casual on Friday or any other day of the week.

Even at a party and after spending time in the heat with a herd of cousins and grandchildren, not a drop of sweat dared linger on his brow. His crisp navy-blue button-up shirt didn't show a single wrinkle, and his black pants were still perfectly creased.

Same with his neat and orderly waves of white hair,

parted razor sharp on the left, no doubt trimmed on Friday for this occasion.

The only thing about him that showed any intensity was the socially acceptable paternal glare he shot Betty's way.

"Good to see you, Dad. Happy Easter."

Her father put on a small smile that barely left his lips, much less touched his eyes.

"The same to you, I'm sure. I do hope whatever kept you has been resolved."

Before Betty could come up with another weak answer—or an excuse to escape into the misery outside after all—her mother appeared, obviously ready to jump into the pile-on.

Mrs. Charlene McHale Compton was as properly turned out as her husband, though she'd chosen a soft, peachy pink for her just-past-knee-length skirt and sunshine yellow for her demure blouse.

Her shoulder length waves were discreetly assisted in retaining their original brunette shade, but hardly anyone besides her children—and presumably her husband—would know that.

And none of the them dared point it out.

"Oh *there* you are, Betty. I see you decided to dispense with proper attire in favor of... Would that be comfort? Or simply what was both clean and available? It *is* clean, isn't it, dear?"

"Clean enough, Mom. Especially for an emergency situation where a friend needed my help."

"Well now, we wouldn't want to disappoint a *friend,* of all people. The rumor here is that *Travis* managed to seize far more than his fair share of your attention yet again. But then again, your attention does seem rather challenging to command as of late. For anyone besides your *friends* or your... And where is Lee today?"

Bless her heart for all eternity, Pearla chose that moment to dart across the living room and sit at Betty's feet, staring up at her with eyes full of impatience.

"Lee's visiting her own family for the week. This is Pearla, Mom. The cat I rescued a little while ago. I had to pick her up from her grooming appointment this afternoon and there was some trouble. Nothing that won't get sorted out."

The typical Charlene Compton disbelieving gaze met those words, and Betty braced herself for whatever verbal weapon would be called into service next time.

"Thank goodness for small favors, I suppose. Sadly your father and I must leave soon, so I hope you'll excuse our rudeness."

Betty smiled, wondering if her effort was as pathetic as her mother's.

And she decided she didn't much care.

She bent to pick up Pearla, holding the soft, rumbling chest against her ringing ear.

"I'll let the two of you get going, then. Enjoy the rest of your day."

Betty deliberately turned away, cradling Pearla in

her arms like a sleepy, rumbly furball of eternal judgement.

She didn't have to see to know her father stood watching, his face a mask of preemptive disappointment.

The people who'd inexplicably been responsible for her entry into the world took the time to speak to everyone else in the room, all while pointedly refusing to so much as glance toward Betty.

Betty herself counted that as a victory.

She wasn't the only one who let out a relieved sigh when the door closed behind the elder Comptons.

Katie materialized by her side and shivered. While she hadn't disappointed their parents quite as much as Betty had, Katie's insistence on continuing her career rather than staying home to concentrate on raising their grandchildren remained a source of contention.

"You think they ever stop wondering where they went wrong with us?"

Betty snorted, regretting it when Pearla jumped in her arms.

"I'm quite sure they're not wondering that about *you* right this minute. They're too busy focusing on *me*. In other words, you owe me one."

"I would have thought having the party here today took care of that. *Any*way, you can't dodge telling me what's going on with Travis any longer now that they're gone. And whatever you put a bug up Stacie's backside about. She's just about pushing her parents and everyone else out of the backyard so we won't have to worry about more interruptions from our nosy elders."

A few more high-powered mimosas and many more rapid-fire questions from Stacie later, Betty didn't feel any closer to helping Travis. Mainly because telling him that her toxicologist cousin refused to speculate without more evidence, while reserving the right to be very curious about what would show up on the missing mug, didn't sound the least bit reassuring.

Katie followed her long-established refusal to slip into attorney mode for even a second during a party, or when it came to a case she wasn't directly involved in. Betty generally respected that stance, but right then she wished her sister would chime in at least a little bit.

But between being able to relax and see Pearla wrap every person in attendance around her precious little toe beans, Betty at least felt like she'd be able to face whatever came next.

Which in retrospect, she should have known was a truly foolish burst of optimism.

CHAPTER 10

DESPITE HER DETERMINATION TO avoid the cat Emporium and all its drama altogether the next day— along with avoiding people as much as possible—Betty found herself sitting in the lobby beside Travis the next morning.

None of the buzz and excitement of a typical business day surrounded them, and she heard none of the happy purrs or outraged howls of cats in various states of spending time away from home, and potentially in water.

The whole building seemed to have taken on a general air of stuffiness and disuse overnight, though that might have been Betty's imagination. Having all the lights out didn't help, any more than the clammy humidity already creeping in with the air conditioning left off overnight.

According to Travis, the first groomer who arrived

to check in the earliest drop-offs normally took care of that.

Not that a business closed because of a police investigation had much of a chance of appearing or feeling normal.

But none of that meant Betty could manage to say no to her friend when he made it clear things were even farther from normal than they had been, especially for him.

With the advance notice of Travis sending her a very early text message basically begging for help, Betty managed to avoid the extremes of her discarded family-approved Easter apparel and the borrowed scruffy t-shirt and shorts she'd washed and brought back to him.

Instead she wore her own far more comfortable navy-blue yoga pants and a matching blouse.

Travis hadn't fared nearly as well, wearing the same denim shorts from the day before and a green tank top that looked like he might have slept in it. His at-all-angles hair only reinforced his unusual state of disarray.

But neither they nor the building itself came close to the disaster of Joey's ransacked office.

No matter what the police eventually said—when they finally got around to saying *some*thing—Betty was more convinced than ever that Travis was right.

Joey's death was no accident.

And someone wasn't satisfied with him cooling his heels over at the morgue, either.

The sharp scent of brewing coffee pulled her out of

her gloomy thoughts. She didn't realize Travis had started a drip coffee maker hidden behind Cortney's desk until he got up.

"No one mentioned there was coffee right here yesterday," she said.

"That's because it's crappy coffee. Why do you think I brought my own yesterday? But this will do in a pinch."

Betty joined him, and the sight of the ancient coffee maker convinced her he was right.

The white plastic body was more yellow now, and from the harsh smell, she doubted it had been properly cleaned in ages. She decided not to glance at the bag of coffee itself so she'd never have to know how long it had languished out of sight.

"What do you think happened back there?" she said.

Travis frowned as he grabbed two white mugs from a shelf under the sputtering machine.

"You know as much as I do. Someone destroyed the place. Not a damn thing left on the shelves or in the drawers, and we have no way to know whether *all* of it got tossed on the floor or not. The only person who might be able to tell isn't around anymore."

Betty held her cup out for him to fill, hoping a good supply of cream and sugar or something would be stashed nearby. She didn't have to taste it to know it wouldn't live up to typical kitchen fare, much less coffee shop quality.

"Any idea who all might have a key besides you? Or reason to do something like that?"

Travis shrugged as he filled his own cup. Thank goodness he next produced ordinary round cardboard containers of powdered creamer and sugar.

"Since none of the entrances were damaged, someone else must have a key. Or they're a lot better at breaking in that I am. My skills in that department stop at getting into Joey's office. Get a chance to share my tale of misery and woe with your sweetheart last night?"

Pretending the creamer and sugar hadn't been terribly clumped, Betty stirred her now beige coffee.

"I told her the basics, yes. She sends her sympathy and a virtual hug. I hadn't met everyone here, but I have a hard time imagining one of his employees did this. I guess it's possible, though."

"I think I met all of them." Travis took a cautious sip, grimaced, and added more creamer. "They were an awfully tight-knit group for something like this to happen, even after only a couple of years. But like you said, wouldn't be the first time. I'll ask Tasha about that and the keys. She's Joey's wife. His widow now, sick as it makes me to say that out loud. Cortney might know more, if she's calmed down. Assuming she *can* calm down, since she's probably out of a job now."

Betty sipped her own concoction that now tasted more like some kind of cheap candy than anything that came from a coffee bean.

She leaned over the desk and glanced around. A

credit card machine sat tucked against a neat stack of cat-decorated carbon receipts that might never get used.

The orderly arrangement stood in painful contrast to the mess in Joey's office.

"That's the other thing," she said. "Cortney didn't know how, but I'm sure the usual receptionist handled cash and checks up here as well as credit cards. Someone breaks in and doesn't even look for any of that? Banks weren't open yesterday for deposits, either. And with all the confusion and everyone scrambling to pick up their cats, I doubt anyone got to do anything like a bank drop. Something's off here."

Travis grunted and reached for the coffee pot again, and Betty was startled to see he'd already finished the foul brew.

"Did you sleep at all, Travis?"

He half-smiled. When he looked at her, the angle of the sunbeam shining through the front door made it clear how puffy his eyes were.

"I laid my head down on the pillow for a while. Does that count? Honestly, I was down here for a good hour before I sent you that text. Tasha asked me to keep an eye on the place and I wasn't about to say no, so I figured the ass-crack of dawn was as good a time as any. When I saw his office..." He shook his head and poured another cup. "The truth might make you think less of me."

"After all this time? I think I've experienced enough

of your twisted side and sick sense of humor that I can handle it."

He held up the mug and took a swig without adding anything to it.

Betty managed not to shudder.

"I stood there looking at the mess, at what some asshole just had to do even after *murdering* him, and I was so furious I couldn't see straight. Not at the killer asshole, not right then."

He rubbed his mouth for a few seconds before going on.

"I was furious at *Joey*. Because I'd just waltzed my own ass right in here, and I knew, I *knew*, there was no chance of a security system or camera or anything else getting me. Because he never bothered to get any of that. If he had, maybe none of *this* would have happened."

Betty put her foul beverage down and hugged him tight. He squeezed back even harder.

"Listen Travis, what if he *did* have all of that security stuff here? Then whoever did this might have gone to Joey's house instead. That could have been an even worse situation, especially for Tasha."

Travis closed his eyes for a second before he nodded.

"I guess so."

"And I'm damn sure I'm not the only one who will tell you it's more common than you think to be mad at someone who... Who passed away. Common enough that I'd say it's actually normal. So don't be too hard on yourself, okay?"

He rolled his eyes, but the half-smile was back.

"Okay. I'll do my best. Guess I'd better let the police know about what happened in Joey's office. Even though that might get a little tricky, explaining how I knew in the first place."

"Want me to make an anonymous call?" Betty said. "I doubt they'd recognize my voice. You didn't touch anything in the office, did you?"

"Nope. About all I could manage was staring at the mess without sobbing. The only thing I might have wanted was that stupid Windy City mug, and it's still missing. Tasha hasn't seen it either. Not that she gives a shit about anything like that right now."

He finished his "coffee" and picked up Betty's half-full mug.

"Sorry, this really is disgusting. Let me go wash these out and dump the rest." He somehow arranged both mugs and the carafe in his hands before calling back over his shoulder. "Call if you want. Or maybe we should go to a payphone instead. You know, in case someone's listening."

Betty rolled her eyes but didn't say a word about yet another worry she truly didn't need.

CHAPTER 11

Betty busied herself straightening up the hidden coffee station, not wanting Cortney or anyone else to come back to a mess. If they got to come back at all.

Upset as she was to possibly have to find a new place to meet Pearla's required adoration and beautification quota, everyone who worked for both the East Lake Feline Emporium and Joey's dog grooming business were probably going to have it a heck of a lot worse.

"I think I'll make that call myself after all," Travis said as he walked back into the lobby. "Tasha did ask me to stop by, and the police talked to me yesterday."

Betty didn't want to admit it, but she was more than a little relieved to leave that chore to him.

"Maybe they'll know something more about what happened anyway. From whatever tests they were running."

He smiled, and the sadness almost lifted from his face for a second.

"See, that's why I like having you around. You give great perspective. But seriously, do you need to get going? I kinda hijacked your day before you were awake enough to tell me to shove it."

Betty waved her hand and smiled.

"Freelancer, remember? And Lee's out of town. I always schedule a recovery day right after I spend time with my parents. I could see who the text came from, so I could have ignored you if I didn't want to be here."

Travis rubbed his forehead.

"That's right, I forgot all about you seeing the parents yesterday. And here I am eating into your well-deserved recovery time. They'll have even more weaponry in their arsenal of reasons not to like me. Did everything go okay?"

"It went as well as it ever does. About the only time I agree to big events with them these days is when Katie hosts. She's always been way better than I am at keeping them occupied and distracted. I *will* tell you they gave me a hell of a time about my casual attire before they left. But I didn't out you as the one who gave it to me. But they do know you usurped some of their required parental critiquing time. Again."

Travis's soft laugh as he picked up the desk phone relieved a little bit of Betty's worry about him.

"I'm glad I helped give Walter and Charlene something new to fuss about. I'm sure their usual routine or their opinion of me hasn't improved much since I last saw them. Sincerely, if you need to head out, I'll be fine."

Betty shook her head and sat in one of the cat-cushioned chairs.

"Now if you'd said 'I'll be okay' or 'I'll make it' or something honest like that, I might have believed you. Nothing about this is *fine*. Anyway, I got the strong feeling Pearla very much wanted the house to herself. She's still mad at me for exposing her to my parents, which I don't blame her for. I'm afraid you're stuck with me, Travis."

He held one hand over his heart and lowered his head, then looked up into her eyes. His were red again, and this time Betty was sure it was from tears rather than exhaustion.

"In that case, I owe Pearla one. I didn't want to come right out and admit it, but I sure could use the company. I'll treat all three of you to something nice once I can focus again."

He dialed and spoke softly, leaving Betty to her own questions about the whole situation. None of which could be answered without a whole lot more information. Not that she was technically entitled to *any* details unless Travis wanted to tell her.

Sometimes supporting a friend through a rotten situation could be almost as hard as going through one herself.

A sharp gasp drew her attention back to Travis, who

stood frozen, the phone's handset clutched against his ear so hard his fingers were going red. When she moved to stand beside him, she saw the muscle of his jaw working even as he muttered affirmatives at whoever he was listening to.

"No, I can't say I was surprised," he said. "I'd appreciate it, and I know his family will, too."

He needed a couple of tries to get the handset back into place.

"I'm guessing they didn't say anything you didn't expect."

"You're wrong there, at least about part of it." Travis blinked several times. "No one thinks this was any kind of natural causes now. But I didn't expect what they found, and neither did they."

"Some kind of exotic nerve agent? Or a brand-new thing they've never seen before?"

Travis picked up the sugar and creamer cannisters and set them in plain view on Cortney's desk.

"Nope, not even close. Cyanide. Freaking *cyanide*, which is absurdly easy to detect these days. Whoever did this wasn't even pretending to try to keep what they did secret. They might as well have walked in the front door in broad daylight and shot him with a dozen witnesses and a film crew."

Betty eyed the canisters uneasily.

"I'm so sorry, Travis. That sucks, even if you were waiting for it. What are they going to do next?"

"Send another crew back to investigate with that in

mind. Don't worry, I have no reason to think the poison was in these nasty old things. No more than the original ingredients are, anyway. But they asked me to make sure anything I touched is available so they can match my prints if they need to. Better that than finding them by surprise and having to backtrack."

"Guess they'll need mine too, then, since I touched those. Do they think the killer wanted to get caught?"

He shook his head and stared at the ceiling.

"They're not giving much away, at least not to me. I'd say the killer doesn't give a damn about getting caught. That or they think they're too smart for the police or anyone else. My guess is making sure Joey was dead mattered more than anything else."

Betty shivered at the chilly, final sound of his voice.

"I know the investigators will ask you this, but now that you've had a sleepless night to brood about it, do you have any idea who? Or why?"

Travis met her gaze, and his expression was as cold as his words.

"Nothing worth wasting time with. But someone does know, or at least has an idea of where to start. I've got to talk to Tasha about the mess in his office anyway. Like you said, the police will do the same. But I wonder if I might know about people in Joey's life that she doesn't."

CHAPTER 12

MUCH AS BETTY wanted to support Travis, she wasn't
thrilled when the investigating officers decided to interview the two of them separately almost as soon as they
walked in the Feline Emporium's door.

They were more subtle about it than that, of course.
It was easy enough to ask Travis to walk back with one
to look at the mess in Joey's office, while the other
waited out front to keep Betty company.

She watched as a middle-aged man with a neat gray
goatee walked Travis back to the destroyed office, then
turned to the female officer staying behind with her in
the lobby.

Detective Cheryl Markov appeared to be around
Betty's age, with a short cap of red hair and lively gray
eyes. Her smile seemed kind enough, almost apologetic.
She wore forest-green trousers with a lighter blouse that
would have fit into almost any office culture in the city.

But Betty had seen too many TV and movies to make the mistake of thinking the detective wouldn't be paying close attention to every word and gesture during this supposedly spontaneous interview.

And she was downright angry at being separated from Travis. She was tense and nervous and tired, but she couldn't help feeling the implication that the police thought he was somehow involved in what happened to Joey.

Her parents would have been delighted to agree, and to make damn sure everyone around them knew it.

"Sorry to keep you here, Ms. Compton. I know this is a stressful time for everyone involved. My partner should be back out soon with your friend. How long did you know the deceased?"

Betty shook her head. "I didn't know him at all. I brought my new cat in for grooming yesterday, but I didn't meet Joey. Mr. Wilkenson. I got here, well, not long after you took him away."

Detective Markov tilted her head and pulled out a little notebook. Betty wasn't surprised to see the page she flipped to already had several lines of writing.

"That's right, it was your friend Travis who knew the victim. Congratulations on the cat. But I'm a little confused about why you're here again today."

"I've been friends with Travis for a long time, and he's been pretty upset. When he saw what happened back there, I think he wanted someone to talk to. That's all."

"Yeah, that part's a little strange, too. Why he was here to begin with. Is he one of the owners of the business?"

Unease squirmed through Betty's belly and chest. She hadn't wanted to say anything to Travis with him so upset, but the fact that he'd let himself into the building was a bad look no matter how she tried to think around it.

"He's not an owner, no. I think he said Mr. Wilkenson's wife asked him to keep an eye on the place. When Travis got here, he saw how the office was messed up."

Detective Markov nodded, then frowned.

"Here's where I'd prefer to take a look around myself and see if there are any signs of forced entry, and I probably still will. The trouble is the two of you have already been inside for a while now, and your friend Travis even longer. If there *was* evidence, it probably wouldn't be worth much to me now."

Betty forced her hands to stay folded in her lap rather than brush at the sweat rolling down her ribs, and tickling badly enough that she struggled to keep herself still.

The rising temperature in the lobby was part of the problem, sure. But the sinking feeling that she'd already said—and done—something wrong made it a thousand times worse.

For the first time, she fell back on her sister's advice if she ever got arrested.

"Am I under interrogation, Detective Markov?"

The detective held up her free hand and shook her head.

"Absolutely not, Ms. Compton. You're not under arrest or at the police station, are you? We're just having a conversation. That's all."

"So I could stop talking right now, or get up and walk out? And you wouldn't do anything about it?"

Detective Markov leaned forward, elbows on her knees.

"I couldn't do anything, no. All I'm doing now is trying to understand what's going on here, and why the two of you were here this morning. We finished our investigation yesterday, at least we thought we did. Getting the call about the victim's office being ransacked certainly changed things. Having two people wandering around might make it a lot tougher to figure out how to handle whatever happened here."

"I know how it sounds, but we didn't touch anything. I walked into Mr. Wilkenson's office, and Travis did before me. Then he made coffee up here, and took the mugs back to the breakroom. That's pretty much it. Whoever broke in must have done it overnight."

"That's touching quite a few things," Detective Markov said. "So your friend has a key to Mr. Wilkenson's office as well as the front door?"

The humid air wasn't going to explain Betty's flushing cheeks, but she didn't want to draw even more attention by covering her face.

No matter how much she wanted to.

"I don't think he has a key to the office. He said... I guess the door has a trick to it, so you can get in without one. He can explain that better than I can."

"So anyone could walk right in. Or could have overnight. Or before Mr. Wilkenson ate or drank or sniffed whatever sent him over to the morgue. But with the two of you going back there, finding fingerprints is going to be a hell of a lot tougher."

Betty pointed at the sugar and creamer on the desk, hoping her voice wasn't too loud.

"That's why those containers are there. We both touched them, and Travis thought you might need to get our fingerprints. So you'll know them if you find them in the office."

She heard how strange the reasoning was, from a law enforcement perspective, before she finished talking. Like she was trying to justify their fingerprints being all over the place, and reassuring the police not to worry about that.

You know, just ignore any signs of herself or Travis being all over the crime scene.

Detective Markov's narrowed eyes confirmed her fears.

"And exactly how many fingerprint kits do you think we'll need, Ms. Compton? Is there any potential evidence the two of you *didn't* contaminate? Or remove altogether?"

Betty wasn't sure whether anger at the accusations or

her fear for Travis took over, but she welcomed the challenge. For one thing, the hotter emotions gave her a chance to get her fear under control.

"I'm sorry, Detective Markov. I know you're simply doing your job, and one I appreciate you for taking on. But I'm *not* sorry enough to let you say rotten things like that about me or Travis without pushing back somehow. We were *both* careful not to touch anything. As far as either of us can tell, everything is still here if you're willing to sort through the mess on the floor back there. And as far as *I* can tell, you're spending time asking me questions while no one is any closer to knowing who killed Joey Wilkenson."

CHAPTER 13

BETTY STOPPED FOR A BREATH, realizing how loud her voice had gotten and how fast she'd been speaking.

All the tension of the past couple of days had come to call all at once, along with years of frustration over her parents being determined to dislike Travis.

And all of that in front of a police officer who already seemed suspicious.

Even if Betty wasn't quite sure why.

Detective Markov raised one eyebrow and sat back, and it felt like she was examining Betty under a high-powered microscope.

"I'll certainly keep that in mind going forward, Ms. Compton. As long as you keep in mind the fact that I'm not writing anyone off as a suspect just yet."

The chill of her words got through to Betty even in the uncomfortably hot room.

And she wished once again that her attorney sister had been willing to offer any advice during the party the day before.

"Do I need to have a lawyer advising me before I say anything else, Detective? Or does Travis?"

Detective Markov shrugged without looking away from Betty's eyes.

"Only you know the answer to that. For yourself, anyway. As for the person who was in the victim's office before dawn the day after a murder, for reasons he hasn't yet made clear, you'll have to *ask* him yourself. In the meantime, I'd certainly appreciate it if you stay out of here until this matter is settled. Maybe pass that along to your friend? Or else let me know if he decides to pay another visit on his own?"

Betty tried not to scowl, but she doubted she kept much to herself.

"Okay, I understand the mess in the office changed things. But as of yesterday, there was no reason for Travis or anyone else to stay away, was there? His friend —who he lost, *yesterday*—gave him a key to the building. I'm not seeing why it was wrong of him to stop by."

Detective Markov stared at Betty, head tilted to one side. Then she flipped a couple of pages back in her notebook.

"Think he was looking for something in particular? Like maybe that missing mug? The one he told us about when we spoke to him the first time. From what I understand it was hardly a valuable item, though it is kinda strange for something like that to disappear on the same day it seems Mr. Wilkenson died from poisoning. Even stranger for your friend to be so focused on where it might eventually turn up."

Betty rubbed her eyes, wishing she could talk to Travis for just a few seconds. So he could make all of this make sense, or at least explain why it didn't.

And regretting that she'd talked to Detective Markov for so long.

"All I know is he told me the mug was missing when we were here yesterday afternoon. Since he already knew that, I doubt he would have been hunting for it this morning. As far as I know, he stopped by today to check on his friend's business, like I already told you. I don't have any reason to think otherwise. The rest you'll have to talk to him about. Seems to me he might need that attorney after all."

Betty heard what had to be the door of Joey's office, and low voices in the hallway.

Detective Markov flipped her notebook shut and eyed Betty again.

"Maybe he does. I suppose that all depends on whether he decided to cooperate or not. Something you might want to keep in mind, Ms. Compton."

Travis's eyes widened when he stepped into the lobby, probably from the steam billowing out of Betty's ears. At least that's how she felt.

He probably read her mood on her face as easily as Office Markov surely had.

"Everything good out here?" He walked quickly to Betty's side.

"Just *peachy*." Betty hoped her voice wasn't as sharp and prickly as her mood. "Figure out anything new about who might have broken in back there?"

Travis drew back and blinked, letting Betty know she hadn't fooled anyone.

"Not yet. Detective Mays is going to get a team back over here for more fingerprints, since someone touched just about everything after they last checked." He waved toward the sugar and creamer cannisters. "Those have our prints from just a little while ago if you need them for reference."

Betty couldn't help glancing at Detective Markov, who stared right back.

"Yes, Ms. Compton mentioned those to me," she said. "I'll make sure the techs know."

She held out a business card, and Betty took it without thinking.

"In case you remember anything you want to talk to me about."

Betty smiled with her lips pressed together, not giving a damn how it looked.

"I'll make sure I keep that in mind, Detective."

This time the other detective raised his eyebrows, and Betty knew they'd be comparing notes as soon as she and Travis cleared out.

"You've got my numbers," Travis said as he and Betty headed toward the door. "I'll be with..." He blinked and shook his head. "I was going to say the co-owner. I'm meeting Mrs. Wilkenson for lunch, so I guess I'll be with the *owner* in case you need either of us."

CHAPTER 14

As soon as the door closed between them and the detectives, Betty let out her breath in a harsh rush, and not only because the day's damp heat landed like a layer of soggy towels all over her body.

"What happened in there, Betty?"

Betty only shook her head and kept walking. She didn't stop until she was inside her car with the A/C cranked and Travis in the passenger seat.

"I didn't want to say anything where we might be overheard," she said, glancing in the rearview mirror. "I'm pretty damn sure I already said way too much."

Travis shifted sideways in his seat so he could look directly at her, which Betty wasn't ready for.

"I'm sure you're fine as long as you didn't confess for me or something like that. Seriously, what went on with you and the other detective?"

Betty forced her hands to relax on the still-hot steering wheel and risked a quick look at him.

Instead of a furtive expression or maybe a shifty one, Travis only looked confused.

And worried.

"Officer Markov stopped just short of reading me my rights and hauling me in, I think. She seemed mighty damned suspicious. Of both of us."

"That doesn't make sense." Travis scowled. "All my guy did was ask me about the stuff in the office and whether I had any ideas who might have been after Joey. Think they were going all good cop/bad cop on us? Trying to trip us up?"

"I don't know about that, but I can tell you at least one of them seems at least halfway convinced you were in on Joey's murder. Might want to talk to a lawyer before you talk to either of them again, buddy."

Travis surprised her by not only *not* getting upset, but he actually winked at her.

"Good thing I know one, huh? Even if she didn't invite me to the big Easter bash yesterday."

"Only because you and my parents are like gasoline and flame for some reason I doubt I'll ever understand."

Travis snorted and shook his head.

"I can tell you the answer to that one right now, if you really want to know. It might be good for both of us. I get to clear up a mystery instead of just making one worse, even if it might not make anyone feel better. And you can get an answer instead of a bunch more questions. But I'm not saying another word unless *you* tell *me* if you think Katie would be willing to talk to me about all this mess."

Betty held up both hands.

"I can't speak for my stubborn sister now any more than I ever could. I know she's generally swamped with work, but she's also refused to fall under our parents' anti-Travis spell no matter how hard they stirred their cauldrons and waved their wands. If you know, spill it."

Travis ducked his head, and Betty was mildly shocked to see him blush.

"Before I say anything else, the reason I never told you is because it's just so...deeply bizarre. At least it was to me. Remember the first time I met Charlene and Walter?"

"Well yeah. Mainly because it was the only time they were reasonably nice to you. Nice as they ever are to my friends or Katie's, or our cousins' friends, for that matter. It was at Katie's birthday party, the one we had at the suite at the Braves game."

"That's the one. You were dating Darla, remember? But you thought your parents didn't know that."

It was Betty's time to blush, but this one was more from shame and hurt than embarrassment.

She'd been unreasonably into Darla, and she'd thought the feeling was mutual.

It probably was, at first.

But Betty's fear of coming out to her parents back

then had driven an uncomfortable wedge between her and Darla that was the beginning of the end.

"Hang on, did you say I *thought* my parents didn't know?"

To his credit, Travis now looked miserable himself.

"I did say that. Because your father pretty much ambushed me on the way back from the bathroom during the seventh inning stretch. He seemed pretty eager to encourage…" He covered his eyes for a second, and by the time he looked back up his cheeks were brick red. "He wanted to make sure I knew how excited he and your mother were to meet me."

Betty's stomach and heart seemed to fall through her car and onto the hot pavement, where they surely sizzled themselves into mysterious greasy spots.

"Because he assumed we were dating. That's it, isn't it?"

Travis shook his head.

"I wish that was how it went down. I got the feeling he knew what was really going on with you. But he made it painfully clear how much he'd prefer it if I stepped in and made a respectable woman out of you."

"Or at least a straight one," Betty said, more harshly than she meant to.

"Wait, it wasn't quite *that* bad." Travis touched her shoulder. "I would have told you if he'd been that obnoxious, trust me. It was more along the lines of getting you settled down and married. I can't say for sure whether he would have given the same speech to Darla."

Betty did her best not to spit the words out, and nearly bit her own tongue for her troubles.

"But he wanted *me* tamed, in any case."

Travis held up both hands and shrugged.

"You might slug me for saying this, and you probably should. I wouldn't blame you. I think he was more...worried for you. I know this is horrible before I say it, but I honestly believe he wished things would go as smoothly for you as they did for Katie."

Betty closed her eyes, willing the disgusting coffee she'd forced down earlier to stay where it was. At least until she got out of her car.

Because the bile that surged in her throat was way too sibling-rivalry-flavored for her comfort.

Sibling envy was more like it.

With a bitter chaser of parental favoritism.

"Now *that* I believe," she said. "They never quite came out and said I should be more like Katie, but I got the message loud and clear. Perfect husband, perfect career, perfect house, perfect kids, on and on and on. Then there was the *other* daughter."

She scrubbed her face with hands still too warm from the steering wheel.

"I don't like myself like this, Travis," she said through her fingers. "Jealousy doesn't fit me very well."

"Maybe in this case, it's because that's not what I was trying to say. My brain and my mouth don't exactly have clear communication during the best of times, and the channel is pretty much bricked off right now."

He pulled one of her hands down so she had to look at him.

"Listen, I didn't get the feeling then or any time since that Walter wanted you to be like Katie, or that he didn't like you. It was more that he wanted things to be easier for you. I'll be the first one to back you up and say he utterly sucks at showing it, but he does care about you. He didn't want to see you get hurt, and maybe he could tell you and Darla weren't on the same path. *That's* what I meant."

Betty stared at Travis, trying to fight a tidal wave of mixed-up emotions welling up in her chest.

The whole thing escaped in a dreadfully embarrassing laugh/sob/hiccup.

Thank all her practice in keeping her face neutral at family gatherings, she managed not to either throw up, burst into tears, or dissolve into hysterical laughter.

Bless every last hair on Travis's head, he didn't so much as giggle.

"I always thought Walter didn't *understand* me well enough to like me or not. Which isn't that far off from what you said. I guess Katie probably makes more sense to him. At least on the surface."

"It's a good thing he has no idea what a freak she really is, huh?" he said. "Maybe that's my true role in lurking around the edges of your family. To take on all the weirdo vibes your sister throws off so Walter and Charlene can maintain their illusions."

A pressure-relieving giggle escaped Betty at least, and her distress eased up considerably.

"You mean so Katie can maintain her illusion of relative normalcy. I don't know how we've managed to stay close all these years having to dodge all these piles of parental bullshit like landmines."

"Eh, she passes for ordinary easier than you do. Sorry to dump a whole bunch more crap on you out of the clear blue sky like that."

Betty elbowed him, but not nearly as hard as she wanted to.

"You tried to warn me, though you could have tried harder. And you didn't quite explain why Walter dislikes you so much. Surely not only because you never swept me off my feet, except for tripping me a time or two."

"That's probably because I pretty much told him the same thing you just told me. But not in such polite terms. After he kept on pestering me, I snapped and said something along the lines of if he'd paid nearly as much attention to his own daughter as he was to me, he might not be so damn far off course when it came to your love life or what might make you happy."

Betty's mouth dropped open, and possibly for the first time with Travis, she had no idea what to say.

"I don't think I've ever seen or heard of anyone snapping back at Walter like that," she finally managed. "I doubt my grandparents or any of his teachers ever did. I kinda suspect Charlene lays into him from time to time, but that's about it. No wonder he doesn't like you."

Travis leaned toward her, eyes sparkling.

"Is that a note of pride I detect in your voice?"

"Well, yeah. I guess it is. I'm assuming Charlene witnessed all the excitement, and has never recovered."

"She did indeed. But I got the impression she was more invested in the idea of the two of us dating than Walter was. So she was *extra* disappointed."

Betty shook her head, staring up at the pale gray ceiling of her car.

"Maybe I should have invited you to the party, no matter what Katie wanted. Let you take some of the parental heat off of me even better than Pearla did. And it sounds like both of us need to talk to an attorney about the mess you dragged me into."

Travis peered at something behind her, and Betty turned. Two unmarked police cars were pulling into the Feline Emporium's parking lot.

"That's probably our cue to head out," he said. "I doubt the good cop or the bad cop want us hanging around here while they look for more evidence. I am sorry you got caught up in all this, you know. No matter how glad I am to have someone around to keep me from driving myself crazy."

"Wouldn't be the first time Nina owes me for taking on some of your drama. Listen, maybe I should give Katie a call, see what she thinks about the basics. I'm afraid one or both of us is going to say the wrong thing and get ourselves into real trouble."

Travis put his hand on the door handle, but didn't open it and let the furious heat in just yet.

"I'm buying if she can meet us for lunch. Nina's been busy trying to help Joey's wife Tasha keep it together, but they'll both eventually want to know what the hell's keeping me so preoccupied. The more information I have for them, especially Nina, the better off I'll be."

CHAPTER 15

BETTY WAS PLEASANTLY surprised to find herself, Travis, and Katie seated in a huge, air-conditioned cantina-style restaurant a couple of hours later. Turned out Katie had a firm-wide town hall meeting she was all too happy to avoid, along with her usual interest in anything *un*usual to sink her teeth into.

The cantina's bright, desert-and-cactus décor might be a bit typical, but the food was outstanding and generously portioned. The temptation to sample one of the fish-bowl-sized tequila drinks was damn hard to resist, especially after Katie's enthusiastic review from previous dinner visits.

All three of them made do instead with gigantic glasses of nicely tart sweet tea along with shared bowls of freshly made guacamole, cheese dip, and salsa with more than a polite kick.

Even the tortilla chips were crisp and fresh, and the

low-key Mexican-themed music wasn't so loud the three of them had to shout at each other. The aroma of cooking onions and garlic wafting through the air had Betty's stomach growling despite the starters rapidly disappearing from their tile-covered round table.

Katie met clients there often enough that she'd secured a relatively private corner booth before Betty and Travis arrived, with a groovy red rounded seat that could have held six or seven people comfortably. She'd shed her jacket and gotten comfortable in a sleeveless blouse with her bare feet stretched out along one side of the seat.

Her demand that Travis and Betty give her something to keep her out of the office for as long as possible started off the conversation with a rush.

By the time the whole bizarre story was out, their entrees had arrived. Betty didn't bother pretending her shrimp burrito bathed in vibrant red sauce wasn't the most important thing for several minutes.

The fact that Travis and Katie dug in just as enthusiastically kept any guilt at bay, as did Katie's thoughtful expression as she ate.

"Well, I'm sure I don't have to tell you this," Katie said between bites of her chicken enchilada, "but you probably shouldn't have been skulking around in there so early in the morning, Travis. Even if it wasn't technically a crime scene anymore."

"It turned into a crime scene again as soon as we left," he said. "And yeah, I do wish someone else had discovered the newest mess instead. I'm glad I spared the staff that experience, though. They've been through enough already."

Katie pointed at Betty with a fresh tortilla chip.

"And *you* had every right to be irritated with the way you were questioned, but you might not have done yourself or Travis any favors by letting your temper get the best of you."

Betty deliberately scooped out the last of the guacamole, enjoying her sister's scowl.

"You sound just like our dear maternal unit Charlene, Kates. And you know as well as I do that letting my temper out to play would have meant a lot more than speaking my mind in a case like this. Before you say another word, I already know I told Officer Markov too much."

"Maybe so," Katie said. "And maybe next time, you'll remember to call your lawyer before answering a bunch of questions. But the questions she asked gave us a lot of information, too. No request to answering more yet? Perhaps at the police station?"

"Hell, it's not like either one of us get caught up in murder investigations every week," Travis said, smiling. "So I figure we did all right. No requests for a follow-up, not so far."

Katie nodded, taking a long swallow of her tea.

"Okay, at least that's one good sign, even though it may not last. Now take a minute and think before you answer, Travis. A guess is fine, but anything that runs close to what might be the truth would be better. Anyone come to mind who might be involved? Or any reason that makes sense? Did he keep a lot of money or valuables there?"

"As far as I know, Joey didn't keep a lot of money or valuables anywhere. He and Tasha were doing okay, but a whole lot of their time and income went right back into the businesses. His office was more of a place to stash his toys and other weird things Tasha didn't want around the house. She kept her office at the Dog Emporium a lot neater, but it was still her private domain."

"Okay financially?" Katie said. "Or okay in their marriage?"

Travis shook his head slowly, and Betty recognized his *you're on the wrong path, so watch out* low-key glare. Not that anyone as tough and experienced as Katie had anything to worry about no matter how upset he might get.

"This is one time the spouse isn't a suspect," Travis said. "I can guarantee that. As far as I know, their finances are...*were* good enough to support the two businesses and the two of them. They got a lot done successfully in only a couple of years here. Not yacht territory by any means, but they had enough to get away and relax, and take good care of their employees at the same time."

Katie put down her fork long enough to hold up both hands.

"I'm not trying to say anything bad about either of

them. But any attorney or police officer or anyone else involved is going to ask about their relationship. It's just standard practice."

"Well, the two of them were anything but standard." Travis smiled, and his eyes took on a soft glow. "They only got together about ten years ago, but the second I saw them together I knew that was it. Like they'd been best friends their whole lives from the first time they met. Tasha is hardly a pushover or the kind to fall apart in a crisis. Even so, she's having a hell of a time with this."

"I'm sure she is." Katie touched his arm. "What about the stuff in the office, then? You said a mug was missing. Anyone who'd be likely to want it?"

Travis scowled. "The only ones who probably know about it have ones of their own. We all bought the silly things. Everyone on that trip."

Katie met Betty's gaze, and Betty knew they were thinking of the same thing.

A long-ago family trip that wasn't a pleasant memory for everyone.

"Anyone who might *resent* him having it?" Betty said. "Maybe someone who didn't make the trip?"

Travis opened his mouth, then paused. He blew out through his lips instead.

"I gotta say that's a weird turn in the questioning, Betty. Is there more to that?"

Katie shrugged and waved their server over.

"Since Betty hogged all the guac and I have to order more, I'll let her tell it."

"There's not all that much to tell." But Betty's cheeks heated despite all the years that had passed. "Just me and Katie and a bunch of our cousins planning a trip down to Savannah one summer, when enough of us were out of high school to talk our parents into it. Not that Charlene and Walter were *thrilled* about the idea, mind you. But they didn't want to be the only parents to refuse."

"That didn't stop them from making us call and check in every fifteen minutes," Katie said. "Back when that meant stopping to find a damn payphone."

"Anyway," Betty went on, "we all got so caught up in planning and figuring out how to convince our parents that we made a rotten assumption. Our second cousin Michele never could convince her parents to let her do anything, no matter how many adults were going to be around. They were kind of like our parents in Hulk mode. Because of that, and probably because we were so used to her not getting to do things, we never even asked her."

Betty was relieved when Katie jumped in.

"Michele didn't even find out until the whole thing was over. She wasn't exactly thrilled with being left out, no matter what her parents might have said. So she found her own way to get even. Any time she was at any of our houses, she would wander off when no one was paying attention."

"And somehow all of our stupid Savannah souvenirs ended up ruined," Betty said. "One by one. Not totally smashed, because we could latch on to that and do something. But a snow globe got scratched, or the brim of a hat got broken. T-shirts or postcards got ripped or stained, that kind of thing. None of it bad enough to throw the things away. But she made her point. And she keeps making it. No matter how many times Katie invites her to parties, like yesterday, Michele never shows up."

"So you're asking me whether someone who didn't get to go on our boys' trip to Chicago because we didn't invite them decided to murder Joey all these years later? That seems like a stretch."

CHAPTER 16

Katie pulled the fresh guacamole the server delivered away from Betty and close to her own plate, then grabbed a handful of tortilla chips from the refilled bowl for scooping.

"Not necessarily over the trip," Katie said, "though who the hell can say for sure? Could be about anything. Business, school, neighbor issues, friendships or relationships gone wrong. What I'm getting at is human brains can get pretty damn twisted. More than you want to know. Sometimes a resentment grows itself into a monster before anyone else knows it's there."

Travis selected a tortilla chip of his own and held it, staring into space. Katie offered him the bowl piled high with irresistible spicy green avocado goodness, but he didn't respond.

Betty was sure he wasn't trying to hint or guilt her at all.

He was giving the question every last bit of his attention.

"Honestly, I can't think of anyone. But that doesn't mean much. Close as we were, there could have been all kinds of stuff going on that I didn't know about. Up until he and Tasha moved here, I hadn't lived near Joey since right after that trip. That's one reason we took it, you know? Because we'd all be going our separate ways after graduation."

What popped into Betty's mind then had her wishing she'd taken the chance on at least a small margarita.

"I hate this, but we might need to talk to Tasha." Travis flashed his *back off* glare again, but that one had never worked on her. "No, I don't like it either. And I know the police have probably been driving her nuts when she's nowhere near ready to deal with all of this. But you *do* know her—and you knew Joey—way better than the police do."

Katie grudgingly slid the bowl toward Betty.

"She's got a point. Talking to someone she knows and trusts would probably make remembering easier. That and she might remind you of something. Didn't you say your wife has already been spending time there?"

Travis nodded, tilting his head from side to side at the same time.

"Yeaaaaah, Nina's been with Tasha pretty much nonstop since it happened. One thing about Tasha is she's tough as stainless steel. Nina says she hasn't so much as sniffled this whole time. Not that she's not upset, before you start that line of questioning again, Katie. She's absolutely furious. That's what I mean by her having a hard time. Tasha is so angry she can barely function. But that won't last forever. Then I expect she'll have new reasons she can't function."

He let out a long, slow sigh.

"Which might very well mean she'd feel better if she could talk to someone she trusts, who knew Joey, and who's almost as pissed off about this whole nightmare as she is. And who's determined to do something besides keep dusting his office for fingerprints they're apparently never going to find."

Betty used a big chip to shovel out a generous serving of guacamole for herself, then pushed the bowl back toward Travis.

"Okay then, sounds like we have an idea of where to go next. Assuming you're up for it, Katie."

She knew the tease hit home by the way Katie stared wide-eyed and confused for several seconds. Then she scowled.

"Oh no, *please* don't keep me out of the office and their endless rah-rah meeting and the obligatory after-meeting dinner and drinks. I'm dreadfully afraid of missing a single second of self-congratulation and back-slapping. Of course I'm up for it. But only if Tasha is too."

"All I can do is ask." Travis stood, pulling out his

phone. "You know how Nina is with things like this. She's glad to help in any way she can, but the truth is I'm sure she could use a break. And since I've been obsessing over the office and *not* helping with Tasha, I'm the one who should give her that break."

After walking away for a quick conversation—and leaving time for Betty and Katie to finish most of the guacamole—Travis sat heavily and nodded.

"Tasha is fine with talking to you. And my darling bride thinks sooner would be better. Apparently Tasha is still running on anger, but cracks are starting to show around the edges. The dam might break sooner than expected."

"What do *you* think, Travis?" Betty said. "Will we help or hurt, showing up and asking her a bunch more questions?"

He grabbed one more chip and scraped the bowl clean, then chased it with the last of his tea.

"I think Tasha would feel a lot better now talking to someone, actually doing something to try to figure all of this out. And she'll feel a lot better after this all hits her, knowing she at least made an effort before things fell apart. I'm ready when you two are."

He started to get out his wallet to keep his promise to pay, but Katie smacked his shoulder.

"Oh no you don't, buddy. The firm gives us an expense account for a reason. And it's the least I can do to thank you for rescuing me from an afternoon of torture. I'll get this, and we'll get going."

CHAPTER 17

I F BETTY DIDN'T KNOW BETTER, she might have thought Tasha Wilkenson had simply had an annoying day at work rather than losing her husband the day before.

She ushered them out to a lovely glassed-in back porch, complete with a round white table surrounded by chairs with overstuffed pink cushions. A pale-green pitcher full of ice water waited, along with little matching dishes piled high with small cookies of all shapes, sizes, and flavors.

The aromas of vanilla and cinnamon made it clear some of them were baked not that long ago.

Her navy-blue blouse and charcoal-gray pants looked a little wrinkled, but otherwise they would have fit right in at Katie's uptight law firm. Even her red hair was corporate-neat in its braid twisted into a bun on top of her head.

The biggest sign of Tasha's true situation showed in the red rims of her blue eyes, and that could have easily been because of the overabundance of yellow pollen collecting against the porch's windows. A colorful explosion of flowers and blooming trees in the big backyard explained all the vigorous signs of spring.

She hugged Travis hard before offering Betty and Katie a warm two-handed grasp.

Betty was struck by how cool Tasha's hands were, even in the air-conditioned comfort of the porch.

"I know you just came from lunch," Tasha said in a flat, no-nonsense Midwestern accent. "Or I would have put out a lot more. We don't know a whole lot of people in the area, but enough have stopped by to drop off stuff that I have enough to feed a good-sized high school. If there's anything at all you need, just say the word. I so appreciate you taking the time to talk to me. I'm sure the police are doing their best. But they don't seem all that interested in keeping me up to date on what's happening."

After that flurry of words, she pressed her lips together as if she was determined to keep a lot more inside.

Betty took the opportunity to pour water for everyone while they settled into the seats.

Travis put his hand on Tasha's shoulder for a few seconds.

"We're fine, Tasha, thanks for bringing out so much.

I know you've heard me talk about Betty, and this is her sister Katie. Is Nina around?"

Tasha covered her mouth for a second, and Betty spotted another sign of her distress. She'd picked most of her deep pink nail polish off, leaving only a few bits around her cuticles.

"That's what I forgot to tell you. Nina went to the grocery store. She's helping me more than I can ever repay her for. Even with all the food, we're almost out of coffee and tea and milk and juice. Otherwise I would have brought out more than water. Can't possibly go through all of this without enough caffeine to offset all the sugar."

She wrapped both hands around her water glass, closed her eyes, and let out a long breath. When she focused again, her eyes were less red, and the anger came through loud and clear.

"Okay. What can we do?"

Betty was amazed at how different Katie's demeanor, her expression, even her voice came out. She'd never actually seen her sister in the practice of law rather than hearing her complain about it.

Besides recapping everything they'd talked about over lunch, Katie somehow managed to sound equal amounts reassuring, compassionate, and more than a touch angry about the situation herself.

By the time she finished, Tasha leaned forward, and the light in her eyes had shifted from furious to determined.

"As far as anyone connected to that boys' trip to Chicago," she said, "Travis is right about that being the wrong path to follow. Of course the police haven't even gotten that far. One of them keeps mentioning random attacks, as if someone might have *randomly* let themselves into Joey's office without living a single damn fingerprint. I think they don't have any idea of where to go next, so they're already in cover-their-asses mode."

"Whoever did this certainly seems to have planned ahead," Katie said. "And managing to make the plan work without leaving a trace anyone can find makes me think they stayed calm the whole time. Not a pleasant idea, and I'm sorry to say it, but it might help. Remind you of anyone? Any other people come to mind who might have some kind of resentment? Either here or from the past?"

Tasha held her face in her hands long enough that Betty was afraid her emotional dam had reached its limit. She certainly understood why it might.

But Katie only gave a quick headshake, so Betty stayed quiet.

"The building was already a shop before it went on the market," Tasha said, sitting up. "It's not like we took over someone's family home. Both buildings were. So I doubt it was anything about that. We looked around to make sure we weren't too close to other grooming and boarding operations, too. Not that there are many cat grooming operations to speak of no matter where you are. I told the police no one wishes they could remember something more than I do."

Katie picked up a small brown cookie sparkling with sugar. The possibility that it might be ginger worked past Betty's pleasantly full belly to catch her interest.

"This may be a shot in the dark," Katie said, "but did Joey keep a diary or journal or anything like that? Some way to keep his thoughts organized?"

Travis looked up at Tasha and smiled, getting a sad smile in return.

"Travis is your man on that question," Tasha said. "They had a psych class together that got them started journaling for part of their grade. And then..."

Travis waved one hand toward Tasha.

"And then we spent the next many years bugging each other about whether we were keeping up with the practice or not. See, I had a hell of a lot going on right then, and no matter how I hated it at first, keeping that damn journal was probably the only thing that got me through that year. It was like I could extract some of the bullshit, just enough to give my brain room to function."

"And Joey?" Katie prompted before popping the cookie into her mouth.

"Joey wasn't quite as dedicated as I was, at least when it came to word count. Even from the beginning, I'd scribble a couple of regular-sized notebook pages, while he might do a quarter of one page. But he hardly ever completely missed a day, even if it was to write *Standard Level Shit* or *Same Day, Different Dumb* or some other clever nonsense. At least back then."

He turned to Tasha, who logically would know more about Joey's more recent habits.

"Oh, he still kept up with it. Not a lot, like you said, but pretty much every day. I'm feeling kinda dumb myself right now for not thinking of it earlier. When I found out what happened, maybe, or when the police were swarming all over the house."

She hugged herself, the hard lines of her face slipping into shadowy pain.

Her words slowed and her voice softened.

"I never read any of it before, not unless he showed it to me and asked me to. Even then, I always felt a little uncomfortable. It seemed too much like opening a portal into his skull so I could examine his brain. Listen in on his thoughts. I wasn't sure I should see that, or even if I wanted to."

Katie nodded and closed her eyes.

"Feels a little like prowling now, I'd guess." She focused on Tasha. "Makes sense. I promise you I wouldn't ask if I didn't think it might be important. One of my kids keeps a diary, and I think I'd get glared into oblivion if I so much as touched the notebook. But I'd read the whole thing if he was in trouble and I thought it might make a difference."

Tasha seemed frozen solid now, as if the words had

transformed her into a flesh and blood statue. Then she nodded once.

"Joey never asked me *not* to look at them, not once. I think he figured I'd ask if I was curious, which was true. I mainly thought of it as his own private corner, like our offices, or the reading chair I've always had. Excuse me and I'll go grab the last bunch."

Betty finally gave in and grabbed a cookie. Her nose confirmed her guess about its gingery nature.

"Seems like she's doing okay?" she said.

Travis held up one hand and tilted it back and forth.

"She's got herself locked down pretty tight right now. Like her personality is functioning at fifty percent strength or something like it. But I don't think we're making it worse, which might be all we can do."

"Not *all* we can do," Katie said. "Not if I can help her catch one lucky break. And I'm going to do everything I can to make that happen."

CHAPTER 18

BETTY GLANCED AT HER SISTER, surprised at the intensity and tremor in her voice. Katie's eyes weren't as red as Tasha's had been, but her cheeks were flushed and her mouth firm and set. Surely thinking about her own husband and the slow-motion nightmare Tasha had to be going through.

Before anyone said another word, Tasha walked back in with a stack of ordinary spiral-bound notebooks.

Betty ate the cookie to distract herself, and it worked better than she expected. The ginger was sharp and hot enough to balance the sugar and molasses perfectly.

"Joey always wanted exactly the same kind of notebook," Tasha said. "Plastic cover, narrow-ruled, five subject. He liked the idea of getting out his adult problems onto the same paper he's used in high school. He's still got..."

She stared up at the ceiling for a few seconds, then sat, holding the notebooks in her lap.

"There's still a stack of them that haven't been used. Anyway, for what it's worth, I hope these help."

"Whether we find anything that gives us a clue about what happened," Katie said, "I appreciate your trust, Tasha. I'll personally make sure you get them back. Unless you can think of anything else, or if I can do anything at all for you, we can head out. But if you'd prefer company I don't think any of us are in a hurry."

Betty had just decided to keep her mouth shut about approaching deadlines when Tasha shook her head.

"I don't want to keep you. It means a lot to me that you're willing to go to all this trouble."

She stood, and everyone else stood with her.

"I think I'll stay behind if that's all right with you, Tasha," Travis said. "See if Nina has anything for me to do. Or if you do. I'll just walk Katie and Betty to their car."

Betty and Travis had ridden in Katie's minivan since the restaurant was on the way back toward Katie's house.

Tasha's smile made it clear she didn't really want to be alone after all.

"That's fine with me. I'll be right here."

Once they were in the van with the A/C on high

and Travis temporarily perched in the back, Katie groaned and shook her head.

"I know all the theories about how people deal with sudden grief. Hyperfocusing on something else, turning into everyone else's grief counselor, sneaking off for a dose of some drug or drink. But I still don't see how she's holding it together so well. I'd be a hot sobbing mess, probably curled up on the bathroom floor for at least a week. Or I might be the one who breaks everything I can get my hands on while screaming my voice away."

Betty kept her opinion of how efficiently Katie would probably get herself through such a massive crisis to herself. Growing up under Walter and Charlene's roof had given both of them an unusually deep stock of coping mechanisms, some very much on the unhealthy side.

She decided not to mention how badly she thought *she'd* deal with the same situation herself.

"Being this calm can have a dark side for certain," Travis said. "From what I've seen and lived through myself, it tends to make the eventual crash that much harder. Thank you for talking to Tasha, and for whatever you decide to do with those notebooks."

Katie turned in her seat to look Travis in the eye.

"Do you want to read through them instead? You knew him, and neither one of us did."

Travis picked up one of the notebooks, this one with a dark green cover, but he didn't open it.

"Maybe someday. Right now I think I'd be the second worst person to do it. Too close. That's probably why Tasha handed them over so easily."

"I'll dig in this afternoon," Katie said. "Might as well get the billable hours started, even if I decide to do this one pro bono."

"I'll help," Betty said, a bit shocked at the words that had bypassed her brain. "For Pearla's sake if nothing else, and for yours, Trav. And Tasha's. The asshole who did this left a stinking, rotten mess behind. It's going to take more than one of us to clean it up."

Katie stared hard at her for long enough to make Betty uncomfortable, and to kick in her extra-stubborn response.

Yes, she had her own work projects she needed to catch up on. And no, doing legal work for free wouldn't benefit her in any way, besides maybe emotionally if they figured something out.

But she wasn't about to walk away from this, no matter how she'd gotten involved. She was way too caught up in it now.

She probably had been since she stepped inside the East Lake Feline Emporium and saw Cortney's distraught face.

"Okay," Katie said, not sounding happy about it. "I've got a few terms that apply to both of you, though. No more sneaking around a crime scene. And before you argue, I promise that's how your police officer friends are seeing it. And no talking to *anyone* in law enforcement without discussing it with your attorney first. Got it?"

Betty nodded without hesitation, and a beat later, so did Travis.

Katie drummed her fingers on the steering wheel, leaving Betty a little worried about the next condition.

"You may not like this one, but I think it makes sense in this case. We still don't know *why* this happened, and we may not unless we can figure out who did it. Which means we have no idea who's at risk if we get caught poking around. So I'd say no talking to Tasha about anything we find until I give the all clear. Not to hide things from her, or because I think she was involved. The truth is whoever was involved may target her next."

A queasy shiver worked its way up Betty's spine. Partly because the last thing she wanted in the world was for something bad to happen to Tasha. Or for Travis to have to go through yet another loss.

But he echoed a deeper reason for her chill.

"Or I might be next on the list."

"Or me," Betty said in a low voice.

"I hope not." Katie glared at Betty. "But we can't say anything for sure yet, about much of anything. So tell me what we just decided."

"No talking to pretty much anyone without talking to you first," Betty said.

"And no talking to Tasha most of all," Travis chimed in. "Does that include me talking to Nina? Not that we've seen enough of each other to do much talking lately."

A little blue car rolled along the street just then, parking behind Katie's van.

"Never mind," Travis said. "I just answered my own question. Might be time to rethink Nina staying here without me around anyway. Talk to you soon." He slid the van's side door open, then hesitated. "And thank you both."

Betty watched him hurry back and open the car's driver side door. When he caught Nina's tall, sturdy frame in a tight hug, she turned back to Katie.

Partly to distract herself from an unhappy pang of homesickness for Lee.

"I'm ready to get started if you are, Kates. The sooner we can figure out something on this, the better."

"You sure you can push your deadlines this hard, Betts?"

After a glance in the van's door mirror to see Travis still holding his wife, Betty nodded.

"I've got some leeway, and some understanding clients right now."

"Okay then, since we're all in agreement that you and Travis might end up in the firing line here, have you talked to Lee about that possibility? I know you're a grown-ass woman even if the senior Comptons don't, and perfectly capable of taking care of yourself. But I also know I'd wring Greg's everloving *neck* if he got himself wrapped up in a dangerous situation without telling me about it."

"So that means you're planning to tell him about *this* particular situation, then?"

Betty regretted her sharp edge before she stopped talking. Letting her fear and worry—and yes, a bit of guilt for not saying a word to Lee yet—get away with her when Katie was only trying to help wasn't her proudest moment.

"As a matter of fact," Katie said, her voice somehow still calm, "I can't legally tell him about most of the messes I get involved in at work. You know that, so I'll let the snippy tone pass. If all of you agree to it, I will. Otherwise I'll conduct myself the same way I have for decades as a grown-ass woman and cover my own grown ass. Deal?"

Betty leaned her forehead against Katie's shoulder like they had since they were toddlers turning to each other, growing up in a house colder than sitting right beside an air conditioner vent in August.

"I'm sorry. That wasn't fair. I appreciate you getting involved, and Travis does too." She sat up and looked into her sister's eyes. "If I can borrow your living room and get out of the heat, I'll talk to Lee before I do anything more."

Katie stared at Betty for a few seconds, then squeezed her arm.

"Well, okay. Thank you. And of *course* you can borrow my living room. It's not like you ever bothered to ask before, right? Or like you've been in the middle of a murder case before."

She took her own quick peek in the rearview mirror before she started the engine.

"Now, I'm going to insist on paying you, since you'll be missing out on your own work. And doing potentially vital research on a case for me."

"I thought you said this one would be pro bono?" Betty buckled her seatbelt to silence the annoying alarm when Katie put the transmission in drive. "What would you be paying me *with*?"

"Don't worry your pretty little head about that. The truth is every hour you save me will let me work on cases that do bring in the cash. And it sounds to me like we need to have a conversation about how tax write-offs work."

CHAPTER 19

LOVELY AND THOUGHTFUL as Katie's party decorations always were, Betty was far more comfortable when her sister's big house slipped back into normal mode.

Not messy by any means, and not as spare and almost empty as Betty's own house felt sometimes. But no longer anywhere near the pristine arrangements required for Charlene and Walter Visitation (and Judgement) Events.

The pretty pastel and spring-themed pillows and other Easter decorations had vanished back into storage. Ordinary neutral-colored pillows might be tossed randomly on the sofas, or possibly even on the floor.

Cat toys of every description lurked around every corner and behind just about every piece of furniture in the place.

The coffee table in the living room no longer held bowls with neat little piles of candy, but a scatter of books and magazines for kids and grownups alike, and a couple of paperbacks.

Even the homey scent of lemon cookies and other Easter treats had been chased away by what turned out to be a pair of reeking teenaged-boy sneakers hidden behind the sofa. Once those were banished to the garage with much groaning and nose-holding by an embarrassed Katie, a more typical lingering aroma of coffee and popcorn was brave enough to return.

In addition to the rapid exile of the stink-bomb shoes, the coffee table was quickly cleared of all evidence of family life, giving way to Betty's Temporary Journal Research Agency.

Joey's notebooks were arranged chronologically, with the dark blue cover of the newest one flipped open not far from the last entry as she worked her way backward. Betty's appropriately low-tech strategy for combing through them consisted of an ordinary yellow legal pad and packs of tiny little sticky notes for marking any pages that seemed important plucked from Katie's endless supply in her home office, where she had retreated to try to do some work of her own.

And while the cat toys were very much still in evidence, the usually calm-natured kitties had taken themselves to distant locations to avoid the intruder in their domain.

Not their beloved Auntie Betty, especially since she normally brought them a supply of their favorite salmon-flavored treats. Katie's human and feline kids adored Betty in general, treats or not.

But for this visit, besides insisting on paying for the work, Katie wouldn't listen to no for an answer when it came to bringing Pearla along. After all, she'd reasoned in her don't-argue-with-me-attorney voice, Pearla was fairly new to Betty's household, and Lee wasn't home.

That meant leaving her alone for hours at a time, which surely wasn't the best approach.

And she needed to get to know her four-legged cousins, anyway. In a less stressful situation than a full-on meet-the-whole-family kind of party.

The truth was Betty had her own reason for heading home to collect Pearla. Probably not the most honorable reason, but she decided going along with Katie balanced everything out. Especially since Katie was kind enough to remove herself to her cozy home office and close the door.

Pearla had served as a delightful distraction the last time she was in this living room, dreading facing Walter and Charlene. Surely giving Lee a glimpse of their outrageously adorable feline child would make up for a subtle bit of manipulation.

So Betty curled up on the sofa, their designed for the office but perfect for home speaker-enabled phone balanced on the wide, cushioned arm, and hit the button that stored Lee's cell phone number. Otherwise known as a lifeline on a day like this.

Just hearing her beloved Other Mommy's voice over

the surprisingly loud phone speaker had brought Pearla running during previous calls. But just in case, Betty had a little baggie full of the stinkiest meat-scented treats in her pocket.

As soon as the call connected, she couldn't hold back a grin, partly to deny the massive wave of Lee-sickness that threatened to drown her.

And any thoughts of needing a distraction evaporated at the thought of her beloved's face.

She could hear that her sweetheart was somewhere outside from the breeze whistling across the miles. Previous visits to Wisconsin conjured a vision of Lee with the sprawling branches of a still-bare tree over her head and peeks of a deep blue sky showing through. Her hair falling in shining black waves past her shoulders in this vision instead of being strictly contained like it always was from March until October in Atlanta.

Even though Betty knew perfectly well how much further north Lee was, the idea of a green flannel shirt over a t-shirt for the brisk wind still seemed bizarre to her. Even though it would bring out Lee's beautiful green eyes and the warm tones of her dark skin.

"Hey gorgeous!" Lee said, and Betty heard the grin in her voice. "What good deed have I done to get a rare midday call?"

Despite the somber reason for the call, Betty couldn't help giggling.

"Maybe because it's been too many hours since someone called me gorgeous, even if you can't see me. Is it actually cool enough for one of your everlasting supplies of flannel shirt, or is my imagination just tormenting me?"

"Not quite sixty degrees and breezy, which isn't all that unusual for so close to Lake Michigan this time of year. You know you would have been more than welcome to experience the joys of Wisconsin in springtime with me."

Betty laughed under her breath and shook her head.

"I probably should have taken you up on that. Remind me next time, will you?"

"Okay, what's wrong?" Now Betty imagined the adorable wrinkle that would be showing between Lee's curved eyebrows. "And don't tell me nothing, because I can hear it in your voice."

Betty considered deploying her treat-bait so Lee could at least hear their darling's meow, but only for a second.

For one thing, Pearla was currently crouched inside an ordinary cardboard box that had very much not been visible during the big Easter party. Her eyes were half-closed as she gnawed on an already ragged edge.

And anyway, she'd promised Katie she'd talk to Lee. Most importantly, that was exactly what Betty needed to do. Much as she loved her sister and Travis, Lee filled a space neither of them ever could.

"Do you have a few minutes to listen to my tale of woe?" she said. "Well, it's not really mine, but I'm definitely caught up in what's going on. Travis and Katie too."

She heard leaves crunching as Lee walked. In Betty's conjured scene, she sat at a weathered old picnic table beside the thick trunk of the tree, lake visible in the distance.

"For you, I've always got however long it takes. We're just hanging out with a bunch of the grandkids, so Mom and Dad are plenty happy. They both send their love, of course, and so do I. Now let's hear it."

Betty blinked back tears at the thought of Lee's sweet parents actually wishing she was there, and welcoming her with big smiles and open arms, like they had on every visit. Since her own parents hadn't ever really greeted her that way, she doubted they'd manage to get anywhere near warmth with Lee no matter how many years passed.

"I'm really glad you answered, LeeLee. Because I really do need to talk to you. So, when I went to pick up our Pearla girl for the big party..."

Lee listened intently, and Betty knew her wonderfully expressive face was reacting at every weird shift and turn, without interrupting or asking a single question. Not until Betty finally let out a long sigh and said that was it.

So far.

"Oh sweetie, I'm *so* sorry. All that going on and you're there by yourself. And poor Travis!"

Pearla picked that second to leap onto Betty's lap

with no warning whatsoever, scaring a grunt and jump out of her.

"Our girlie here wants you to know I'm *not* alone. And I'm at Katie's right now, so there's that. I'm sure Greg and the kids will be rumbling through here before too long."

Lee held her phone closer and sang Pearla's name, getting a series of chirps and sniffs toward the screen in return.

"You're staying there, right?" she said. "Until this is all worked out or I get back home?"

"I hadn't planned on it. Katie's got plenty going on, and I did used to live by myself, you know."

"That's not what I meant, and I'm pretty sure you know it." Lee's voice conveyed her annoyance perfectly, as usual. "Do you remember what you just told me? That Katie's worried about whoever this asshole is going after Joey's wife, or Travis? If they're paying that much attention, and you've been with Travis and to Joey's house, that's a pretty direct line to our house. And to you."

Betty shivered, and Pearla snuggled into her lap, full of rumbling purrs.

"I kind of hoped you would miss that part. I'm not sure things are that serious. I'm not exactly another of Joey's business partners."

Lee's voice was soft when she spoke, even though Betty could imagine her big brown eyes snapping with worry.

"Okay then, why did Katie want you to call me? And I know you don't exactly obey your sister in pretty much anything, any more than you listen to me about anything. So why did you call?"

"I know. I'm a little worried myself. I got the feeling Travis is going to stay with Nina at Joey's place. Well, Tasha's place now. I hadn't thought about staying here, though. I figured I'd just be careful."

"You're perfectly capable of making up your own mind." Lee said. "And I know you want to keep Pearla safe, even if you don't always think about yourself. So I'll just say I'd feel a lot better if you weren't at home alone, okay? At least until someone has an idea who's behind all of this. Whoever it is doesn't even have touch you, or be around when you are. Joey might not have ever seen who did it."

This time a chill worked its way out from Betty's belly and through the rest of her body. She hadn't actually thought about it that way.

Poison wasn't exactly noisy or high visibility.

"Yeah, you've got a point. I haven't mentioned that to Katie, but I will. Hell, maybe we can all rent a vacation house or something."

Lee finally laughed, and something in Betty's heart rested a lot easier.

"Having some kind of weird murder slumber party sounds about like you and Katie, and definitely Travis. But I'm not sure Pearla's old enough to be exposed to that kind of deviance. At least send me a text and let me know what you're going to do?"

"You know I will. This might sound strange after everything I just told you, but I wish you were here. I miss you."

"With all of that going on I wish *you* were *here.* But I know Travis is needing a friend right about now, so I can deal with how much I miss you. You going to be okay?"

Betty leaned against Pearla's side so she could hear her rumbling purr in one ear.

"I'll be okay now. I'll let you get back to your sane and wonderful family now. Love you."

"They're your family too, so don't try to wiggle out now. They were just on their best behavior for the first few visits while I was winning you over. You don't yet have any idea how deeply weird they can be. Talk to you soon, sweetheart, and I love you right back."

Betty ended the call, closing her eyes and turning her head so she got a face-full of silky fur and warmth.

Yeah, she missed Lee more than ever after hearing her voice. But that few minutes would get her through at least the rest of another long, strange day.

CHAPTER 20

WHEN KATIE WALKED into the living room two hours later carrying two mugs of steaming green tea, Pearla jumped down from her perch on Betty's shoulder, bounced onto the floor, and did her best to trip Katie by twining through her feet and ankles.

Katie had shed her corporate-neat outfit for a loose-fitting pink t-shirt and a pair of purple shorts to go with bare feet. If Charlene and Walter Compton ever saw the extreme casualness of their daughters during a *work* day, they might simply pass out from a serious attack of the vapors.

While Betty had been busy scanning Joey's fairly neat handwriting, Pearla had cautiously, then more boldly, investigated the rest of the living room for herself. Since there were no humans to charm with no party underway, she took every chance to deposit gifts of her white hair across every surface she could reach.

In theory, even if Katie's cats declined to make an appearance to say hi on this visit, they'd at least be familiar with their new cousin's scent and coat color.

"Looks like she's making herself entirely at home." Katie sat beside Betty on the sofa and handed her a mug. "And of course my little demons are displaying perfectly awful manners and ignoring their guests entirely."

Betty held the mug in both hands and breathed in the earthy steam and a touch of what smelled like orange blossom honey.

"I'd never criticize any of my nieces or nephews for being antisocial from time to time. I'm a fairly new cat person, but I get the feeling they socialize even more on their own terms than I do."

"That they do," Katie said. "And kids are even worse. Speaking of little human demons, they'll start straggling home in about an hour. Finding anything?"

"Nothing to speak of yet. Just a lot of stuff about the two of them moving here, getting the businesses set up, figuring out how to get around this sprawling mess of a city. Unless he had another set of super-secret journals hidden away, Travis was right about Joey and Tasha. Joey was crazy for her, and nothing he wrote sounds like she felt differently."

Katie took another sip, then let out a long, tea-scented sigh.

"That's about what I expected. Getting close to

before they got here? Who the hell knows, maybe it was someone from their past."

Betty picked up the open notebook. Most of the entries were indeed fairly short, so more than one date was neatly noted on blank lines between the writing.

"I'm back to right before they closed on the building for the dog grooming place. He and Tasha planned it that way, to get the cat operation up and functioning to fund the dog one. Worked like a charm, and they were both running in the black before long. The two of them made a good team in marriage and in business."

"I can't even imagine working with Greg," Katie said. "Much as I love him, he'd drive me crazy in the first fifteen minutes and I'd end up throwing him out the senior partner's penthouse window. That makes me want to find something even more. I know we can just ask Travis about this, but do you know where they moved here from? Or what they did there? Same kind of business?"

Betty flipped the notebook forward a couple of pages at a time.

"They were all in school together in Ohio, and I think that's where Joey and Tasha met. Near Columbus. He keeps mentioning what worked at their first shop in here, so I think the business was the same."

Her eyes went to one of the frequent one-line entries, but this one wasn't as silly or sweet as the rest.

"So if we *do* find something," she said, "are we reporting it straight to the police?"

Katie stared at Betty.

"Why? Did you find it?" She elbowed Betty, none too gently. *"Why?"*

Betty pointed to the entry.

Happy couple, departing for points south, seeks proper and qualified conjurer to bind evil forces safely inside 270 Containment Zone.

Katie's breath caught.

"I don't suppose you know much about Ohio?" she said. "Perhaps whether 270 is an outer belt like 285 is here?"

"I don't, not unless you have a handy road atlas or map close by. But I happen to know exactly who can tell us."

CHAPTER 21

A QUICK PHONE call brought both Travis and Tasha to Betty's living room, along with another stack of Joey's notebook journals. Betty didn't have to ask how relieved Travis's wife was to take the chance to go back to their house and have some time to herself.

Nina was one of the kindest souls on the planet, as anyone who spent even a little time with her would happily agree. But a few days of grieving-friend-duty was exhausting to even the most saintly of people.

Not willing to lapse in her hostess game even when she was in work-from-home mode, Katie supplied more tea along with a buttercup-shaped dish full of a mix of leftover Easter candy.

Pearla of course went directly to Tasha and curled up on her lap. That was another bit of cat-person lore Betty was discovering the truth of. They unerringly recognized the new person—or the upset one—and generally offered the wonderful gift of their presence accordingly.

With her lap thus occupied, Tasha had the intriguing journal entry on the sofa beside her.

"It never even occurred to me to think that far back when it came to possible suspects," she said. "And I'm not sure it makes sense now. I know Joey was eager to make a change and start over in a new place after so many years in Ohio, but I can't imagine things were that bad for him there."

Katie—perched beside Tasha on the sofa across from Betty and Travis—flipped the notebook over to one of the pages Betty had marked with a tiny note.

"We had a few minutes to keep reading while you two were on the way over. I can't say anything for certain, but it sounds to me like he might have kept a few things to himself. You weren't in business together before you moved here, were you?"

Tasha shook her head slowly as she read.

"Not even close. I ran a boutique near OSU, kind of a gift shop and trinket place working with local artists and such. That's one reason we have so much merchandise in our shops here. Pet people love that kind of thing. I thought... I just thought we made such a big change because he wanted to concentrate more on working with cats and his business partner hated the idea."

"The entries I marked aren't exactly proof positive,"

Betty said. "But with everything else, we figured it was worth asking you about."

"Then it's up to the police to take it from there," Katie said. "At the very least, they'll have something to follow up on, and someone to question. Before we look at the rest, does any of this ring a bell, Travis?"

He stared down into his mug of tea.

"Joey hated worrying you, Tasha, and he did his best to avoid it. Probably more than he should have. So yeah, sometimes I heard the rotten stuff he wanted to get off his chest without putting you through it. But all I knew was he wasn't happy with the way things were going in Ohio, especially at work. He didn't mention how bad it had gotten. Or that he worked with someone who might have turned out to be an insanely jealous psychopath."

Tasha stared at him, looking confused and frightened. When he finally looked up and met her gaze, his heartbreak and anger balanced perfectly on his face.

Betty's own heart ached at the other things Tasha hadn't yet seen.

The truth was the journal entries hadn't simply caught Betty's attention.

They'd chilled her through and through, and set off all of Katie's alarms at once.

Once the dates went far enough back, Joey hadn't only written his thoughts, short and succinct as his entries could be.

He'd also had a habit of sketching in the margins,

and sometimes on the main part of the page. Mostly drawings of Tasha or their pets, and surprisingly good ones at that.

But he'd sometimes decorated his words with darker images.

A closeup of a wreck he'd seen on the interstate a few years back. Nothing overly graphic or gory. But his choice of focusing in on a child's stuffed giraffe in a scatter of broken glass was plenty disturbing.

Another sketch showed a cottage crushed under a huge tree, close by the description of seeing the reality on one of his long walks.

What alerted Betty and Katie was several images of a man's face, with varying expressions of upset.

The earliest—months before he wrote about moving to Georgia—showed eyes and mouth narrowed in annoyance.

As time passed and Joey wrote more about difficulties with his business partner and eventually his difficult decision to leave, the man's expression had gradually shifted to open-mouthed, screaming fury.

Katie flipped the pages again, starting with the mildest drawing.

Tasha drew back, one hand on her chest.

"That's Joey's business partner. Or he used to be. Chris Mason. I don't think they'd talked at all since we left Columbus. Are you saying he might have something to do with all of this?"

Katie covered her mouth with one hand for a second before she went on.

"Joey wrote a lot about Chris. And the drawings changed over time, too."

Tasha's own exhausted and sad face shifted along with her husband's sketches, and oddly along a similar path. But the time Katie got to the most recent drawing of what looked like a madman, Tasha's own anger was clear.

"I'm so sorry to have to show you these," Katie said. "And I'm afraid what he wrote matches what he drew. There was a lot more going on besides a disagreement over how the business was going."

Instead of reading the entries, Tasha turned to Travis.

The freezing cold of her voice when she spoke could have cut glass.

"Did you know about this, Travis? How bad things had gotten with Chris?"

He stared back steadily

"I didn't know any kind of details. Only that their partnership had soured enough that Joey was ready to make a change, even if it uprooted both of you and everything you'd worked so hard to build. He put himself through a lot of hell over that."

Tasha's harsh laugh had Betty blinking back tears.

"I sincerely doubt it was anywhere close to the hell he's put me through over the last couple of days." She covered her eyes with one hand and stroked Pearla with the other. "I know that sounds horrible, I do. I've been struggling with the entirely normal and even more awful reality of being furious with him. And I *hate* it."

She lowered her hand, tapped the notebook page, and turned her agonized glare toward Katie.

"You really think what he wrote about is bad enough to bring this to the police?"

"I think we'd be foolish not to," Katie said. "The truth is they may be struggling to find leads in Atlanta because the killer doesn't live here. If this is the guy, he may not have been around long enough to leave much of a trail to follow."

Travis looked at Tasha with his eyebrows raised.

"But did this guy say anything that sounded that serious? Assuming Joey wrote any of the worst stuff down."

Tasha shook her head and pushed the notebook toward Katie.

"I don't think I'm up to reading what he wrote. Not yet. And I'm not about to dislodge this sweet girl right now."

Katie grabbed the notebook just as both Travis and Betty stood to go get it.

Travis froze before he managed to sit back down, staring at one of the drawings.

CHAPTER 22

"Wait... I've *seen* this guy," Travis said. "I'm sure of it. At the grocery store, and I think at the hardware store, too. Not the ones by my house, but closer to work. A few times over the last couple of weeks."

"Closer to your work," Katie said, "and maybe far away from Joey's?"

Travis nodded, his face a misery.

"Yeah, far enough away that I wouldn't be over there if I didn't work out that way. I remember him because he was humming to himself. In time with his walk. Kind of like he was providing his own theme music, strange as that sounds."

Tasha let her breath out with a soft pop, as if she was practicing how to say the letter *p*.

"It's stranger to hear. Sounds like you met Chris all right. He did that everywhere he went, all the time. Joey told me Chris managed to keep it mostly under control if he was in a job interview or speaking in public or something like that, but otherwise it never stopped. It didn't bother Joey for some reason."

Her voice dropped along with her gaze.

"Maybe because he made the fatal mistake of trusting the guy. Not that any of this explains why Chris would do such a thing. Or even if he *could*."

"I don't want to get anywhere near putting ideas into your head," Katie said. "Maybe you could look for a photo at home, or from an old ad or something like it. A likeness that's harder to deny than sketches, no matter how good they are. Once we can identify him —if he's still here at all—we can let the police figure out the rest. It would be an awfully big coincidence for him to just show up here all of a sudden right before..."

Tasha nodded and rubbed her forehead.

"Right. I may not know how bad things really got between them, but I doubt Joey would have invited him down here without saying a word to me about it. Or that he would have kept quiet once he found out Chris was here. I mean, they were business partners for four or five years. If they were still on speaking terms, Joey wasn't the kind who'd want to miss catching up."

Travis shook his head.

"No, he wasn't. We didn't see each other for years at a time, but if one of us got close enough for a visit, it was like no time had passed at all."

He looked at Betty, and her heart dropped. She was

sure he'd recognized how badly she did *not* want to add to the conversation.

"What else did you two find, Betty? Anything the police need to know about right away?"

She was afraid if she hesitated, or if she let Katie jump in and explain, the guilt would gnaw at her until she drove herself crazy.

That didn't make it any easier to speak to her friend, or to Joey's widow.

"It sounds to me like things got a lot worse than some kind of business dispute. This Chris person was really scaring Joey. Enough so splitting up the partner-ship and even closing the business didn't seem like nearly enough distance. The move was for a lot more than a change of pace. He might have reported Chris to the police himself."

"Here or back in Ohio?" Tasha snapped.

"It's hard to tell from what he wrote." Betty marveled at how soothing Katie's voice was, even though her eyes still sparkled with anger. "It's all in past tense. All I could tell for sure is he wasn't happy about the results."

"Let me guess," Tasha said. "They didn't do anything about it. Which makes me think he contacted them in Ohio. He had trouble around the shop a couple of times, but he never could get anyone to take him seriously. Honestly, I thought that was the main reason he wanted to move. And he *let* me think it."

"That may have been because Joey thought it was

Chris who vandalized the shop in the first place," Katie said. "Maybe trying to get insurance money, maybe trying to intimidate Joey. Neither Betty nor I could tell from what he wrote, but you might be able to. Or you, Travis. He seemed to think Chris was getting into financial trouble, and the stress tipped him over into mental trouble. I know this is all speculation, but do you think that's possible?"

Tasha sat forward, elbows on her knees and face in her hands.

"No wonder the police didn't take the report seriously." She sat up and clenched her fists in her lap. "Not that I don't think Joey might have been right. I didn't know Chris all that well, but he did seem to have kind of an expensive lifestyle compared to us. That's hardly illegal, though. I doubt anyone listened to Joey at all."

Betty thought of Officer Markov with her relentless questions and refusal to pretend Betty and Travis weren't suspects.

"If the detective who interviewed me gets hold of this, I don't think there's a chance in hell *she* won't take it seriously. I got the feeling she was personally offended that no one had found any leads yet."

Katie held up one hand when Tasha started to speak again.

"That's as good a place to get back on track as any. Tasha, you did a hell of a job thinking of these notebooks in the first place, and Betty going through them saved me a bunch of time. I think the best thing we can do now that the two of you have verified who Joey thought was worth sketching several times is bring the police in."

Tasha threw up both hands, and all traces of anger left her.

Now she only looked weary, and heartbroken.

"Of course, that's the only thing that makes sense. You two did a great job putting things together this much. But I'm guessing if this guy knocked on the door of any of our houses, not one of us would know what to do about it. Legally, of course. Since none of us would *ever* take things into our own hands."

Betty was the first to break the cold silence.

"I'd do my best to solve the problem, or I'd want to. And I never even got to meet Joey. I truly wish I had. I agree about the police." She hesitated, not wanting to be insensitive in front of a woman who'd just lost her husband.

Sometimes it was worth the potential pain to get things moving.

"I promised someone I love that I'd talk to them for my own safety. If we *are* dealing with someone who'd travel all the way from Ohio and didn't seem to give a damn who saw him, letting the police defuse whatever he's got planned next is the only thing that makes sense."

Betty watched Travis while she spoke, and she didn't look away after Katie jumped back into her attorney mode. The lines of sadness and anger on his face shifted and smoothed into a calm she didn't like.

"Sounds like we're all in agreement," Katie said. "Unless one of you has an objection, I'd say our next step is to get in touch with the police and go from there." Her professional demeanor slipped and she scowled and pursed her lips. "All right, what is it, Betty? You're biting back something, so you might as well spit it out."

After thinking about it for a few seconds, Betty decided not to bother with trying to be delicate or polite. That was very much the behavior their overly sainted mother would have approved of, anyway.

"What are *you* thinking, Travis? And don't pull any bullshit with me. Not right now."

The resurfacing of his stubborn *back off* glare verified her suspicions.

"Okay, but remember you asked. I'm thinking how easy it would be to hang out where I've already seen the jackass, and solve the problem for everyone. Joey was exactly the kind of guy who'd want to help if he could, and who'd feel guilty if he had to give up and cut someone off. Sounds like he got tangled up with someone who didn't mind taking advantage of his good nature, which is pure freaking evil as far as I'm concerned."

He crossed his arms and sat back like an obstinate teenager.

"Before all of you decide you need to jump in and

talk me out of it, I'm quite sure my wife would remove my head from my neck for me if I actually did it. None of that stops me from wanting to. Or imagining exactly how I'd do it."

Tasha shrugged, and the frozen tone of her voice raised goosebumps all over Betty's arms and legs.

"I wouldn't try talk you out of it, Travis. Not even for a second. About all I'd do is give you my own ideas, and probably insist on helping."

Katie rubbed her hands together and stared at the ceiling, then folded them in her lap. As she spoke, she gazed into everyone's eyes, one at a time.

"I told you all before we got started that I had to be careful with what I said. I'm not exactly your attorney. Not yet, and none of you are obligated to hire me. This is all very general advice. *But.*"

She held up one finger.

"This is even more off-the-record. Got it?"

She waited for everyone to nod. Betty's stomach seemed determined to knot and roll itself right out of her body at the flush and fury on her sister's face, but she kept her mouth shut.

"If I were in your shoes, Tasha, and yours, Travis," Katie said, her voice cold but somehow sympathetic, "I'd want to do exactly the same damn thing. Betty can back me up on how hard it can be to stop me once I get an idea in my head, partly because she's exactly the same way. If someone came after my family, I'd be pure hell to deal with. And, I'm still going to ask you to *please* let the police handle this."

She didn't actually ask for agreement, but Betty wasn't the only one who felt compelled to agree anyway.

"Okay, good." Katie nodded once, the tense lines around her eyes and mouth relaxing a little. "Then how about you call your detectives, Betty? While they're on the way, I'm hoping Travis can put together at least a loose timeline of when he's seen... Let's just call him Joey's former business partner."

A faint smile finally crossed her face.

"And I'll see if I can convince my maniac kids to detour a bit so they won't storm the house with a thousand questions and at least that many weird noises and strange smells before we get finished."

CHAPTER 23

Much as Betty loved spending time with her nieces and nephew—who could indeed tend toward the maniacal side right after school—she was relieved their father whisked them off to an early dinner for a couple of hours.

Because by the time Officer Markov and her partner finished extracting every possible bit of information about Chris Mason from the journal and those who knew him, Betty, Travis, Tasha, and even Katie were exhausted and starting to get more than a little snappish.

And the journal had given up even more of Joey's secrets before it and the others were taken in as evidence.

Turned out he'd been talking to himself about wanting to end the partnership and leave the business for quite a while before the worrisome sketches of

Chris's increasingly angry face appeared. When he finally worked up the nerve to mention the idea in the most vague of terms, the scarily sharp and accusatory response only reinforced the initial fear.

Tasha, ignoring or unaware of the slow stream of tears running down her cheeks, confirmed that he'd gradually introduced the idea to her at the same time. And that he'd kept his true worries to himself, sharing that deeper reality only with his journal.

Detective Markov, her half-finished cup of coffee sitting abandoned on the coffee table in front of her, flipped the notebook closed on her lap and tapped her pen on the plastic cover. Her own much smaller notebook sat beside her on the sofa, several fresh lines taking up more than one page.

Today her dark blue pants and white shirt made it more clear she was a police officer, but her attitude was a good bit less suspicious. At least to Betty's mind.

Maybe because she wasn't the one answering most of the questions in a building where a man had been murdered.

"That's a hell of a lot more to go on than the last time we spoke," Detective Markov said. "And knowing what the suspect looks like and where he's been should make a big difference. I appreciate all of you for the information. Now, what are you going to do to keep yourselves safe while we investigate? We'll do what we can, but unfortunately checking out everything you eat or drink isn't in the department's budget."

That quick zeroing in on Lee's fears and the reminder that a poisoner was still out there sent ice through Betty's middle.

Before she could manage to speak, Katie jumped in.

"Well, I want Betty and Pearla to stay here. This isn't exactly protective custody, and I'm sorry to say this, but it *is* another step removed from this Chris person's awareness. With that hopefully settled, I'm worried about you, Travis and Tasha. You could certainly stay here if you're willing to deal with three extremely chatty kids and cats. They'll all eventually get curious."

"Good," Detective Markov said with a smile. "About curious kids and the possible arrangement. From the kinds of cases you've been involved in, I know you understand basic security. The system you have set up here is a good one. Just make sure to keep it armed."

Pearla of course chose that moment to leap into her lap after making the rounds of everyone else in the room. After a jump and grunt of surprise, Detective Markov rubbed Pearla's head. She didn't exactly seem like a natural cat person, but the effort was sincere.

Betty's opinion of her leveled up immediately.

Travis managed to keep his smile to a minimum.

"Tasha, you know you're more than welcome to stay with Nina and me if we don't all decide to crash here. I honestly don't think the guy was paying attention to me when I noticed him. Otherwise we can both stay with you if you want."

Detective Markov shook her head.

"We can't assume he didn't notice you, especially since you saw him several times. That sounds unlikely if he was trying to keep any kind of low profile. *If* this is our guy—which is nowhere near proven—using poison might mean he won't approach anyone for a physical confrontation. But I'm not willing to rely on that. Wherever you stay, Mrs. Wilkenson, I'd be glad to set up protection. Same for this house as well. I'm sure I don't have to mention taking care with food or drink coming from outside."

Katie paled and put her hand on her chest.

"I'm sure they're fine," Betty said. "Getting all the way to your kids at a restaurant would be a whole lot of steps, right? And Pearla and I would love to stay here if it's okay with your cats."

Katie smiled, but she blinked back tears.

"That sounds like taking on extra worry to me as well," Detective Markov said. "You don't have any kind of history with the suspect, and you just got involved today. How about you all talk your arrangements over and let me know? In the meantime, we'll get out to the locations you mentioned. We might get lucky with security footage and purchases he may have made."

She pulled out several more business cards and handed them around. Her partner did the same, but his amused expression made it clear he knew who was in charge.

Everyone stood up when the two detectives did. Detective Markov motioned Betty to the side. Betty did her best to keep from tensing up with the memory of their last conversation.

"You made the right call on getting your sister involved," she said quietly. "No telling how long it would have taken to connect the dots to the journal otherwise. If you'll let me offer a little bit of advice, I'd still keep an eye on your friend Travis. My guess is he's a lot closer to doing something foolish out of anger than even *he* knows."

Betty watched Travis speaking to Tasha, and the tension in his stance didn't match the compassion in his eyes. She'd known him long enough to recognize that angry set to his shoulders.

"I'll drive him to take Tasha wherever she wants to go, then recruit him to go home with me for supplies. He tends to let me call him on his bullshit most of the time. Not that I can promise he'll listen."

Detective Markov nodded.

"Fair enough. I hope you understand why I pushed you so hard when we spoke before. The two of you showing up at the crime scene wasn't the kind of thing I like to see. Especially not when someone decided to wreck it all over again."

Betty snorted and rolled her eyes. Something about standing out of the way like this—almost like they were invisible and having a secret conversation—let her speak more honestly than she normally would have.

"We didn't make the best choices that day, no. Now I hope *you'll* understand *me* saying Travis probably felt a lot like you did that day. Pissed off at the whole situation, and frustrated that no one seemed to know which direction to go next. I know nothing is solved yet. But feeling like there's at least a beginning makes a difference."

"Understood. We all need to do our best to make sure that progress doesn't get knocked off track by someone acting without thinking." She glanced at Betty, then returned to surveying the room, eyes moving restlessly. "I hope none of you decide to play the hero."

"Not if I can help it," Betty said. But Detective Markov showed no sign of hearing as she walked away.

As soon as the two detectives left, Katie shooed them all toward the door.

"I meant it when I said y'all are welcome to stay. But let me explain that to the kids and my husband instead of them busting in here with more questions than the police had, and a lot less patience. Sweet Pearla is more than welcome to stay, of course. Just bring her cat food and litterbox when you come back so we won't have kitty wars on top of everything else."

CHAPTER 24

DESPITE TRAVIS'S best efforts to convince her otherwise, Tasha insisted on some time to herself at her own house. Betty could see her point after the last few days, not to mention her feeling of safety with the police cruiser already parked out front.

Travis couldn't have been as opposed to the idea as he claimed since the drive back to Betty's house was relatively grumble-free.

Pretty much talking-free too, until they parked in front of Betty and Lee's charming Craftsman bungalow.

Set back from the road with an unusually deep front yard, the forest-green wood siding set off the little islands of yellow, white, and orange daffodils she and Lee had planted a couple of years ago, tucked into tidy rock circles. None of the other flowers dotting the landscape had broken ground yet.

But the hedge of crepe myrtles on one side and

altheas on the other acted like a picture frame even before their shows of brilliant burgundy and delicate lavender got started.

Betty had loved her house since she bought it almost twenty years ago, and almost ten years before she met Lee. Knowing no one was waiting for her inside still made it look and feel desolate to her eyes and heart.

And that made her heart break all over again for Tasha.

"What are you going to do, Travis? And I don't just mean for the next few hours."

He stared out the window toward her house.

"Remember how much fun we had pulling up all the ugly carpet in there? I'm still surprised any of us ever managed to wash all the gunk off our hands and out of our hair."

"I remember. I still appreciate you and everyone else every time I manage to spill something. I'd about a thousand times rather break out the mop than try to scrub a stain out of a yucky old carpet. *And* you didn't answer my question."

He shook his head before finally looking into her eyes.

"I know I didn't. That's because I don't know. I'm not planning to go hunting for this guy to try to beat him with a tire iron, if that's what you're asking. But if I run into him at the grocery store again? I just don't know. What would *you* do if you saw him?"

"Besides call Detective Markov right that second?"

Betty's hesitation surprised even herself. "I hope I'd steer clear. Or better yet, get myself the hell away from him. Lee would probably wring my neck for me if she knew I was saying this, but I don't quite trust myself to say for sure. If it *was* him, he made a huge freaking mess in a bunch of lives for a ridiculous reason."

It was his turn to surprise her by laughing.

"See? I'm not the only one, and I'd be willing to bet Tasha, my darling wife, and even Katie feel the same way. So maybe we should trust strength in numbers like the good detective said. Let's grab your stuff and get some supplies before you go back to Katie's. Even with three kids, I'm sure she didn't plan on feeding a crew today."

Betty snorted.

"There's where you're wrong. Her coffee supplies may run short with extra adults, but I'd swear she shops for her family about once a month and fills her van to the top. We won't make a dent. But taking back extra is a good idea, not to mention the kind of polite behavior Walter and Charlene Compton would heartily approve of."

"In that case, I'm not sure we should do it. I'd hate to break my perfect record of annoying your parents."

Betty took the time to smack his shoulder a good one before getting out of her car.

"You've got a long way to go before you take over the lead in annoying them from me. Come on, let's get back before Pearla decides to move in with my sister permanently."

The second she stepped into the kitchen, Betty knew something was wrong.

Like the rest of the house, the cozy space was decorated with a mix of traditional and modern. Ceramic tile that looked remarkably like oak flooring paired with shiny black appliances, while a shelf full of vintage cookbooks shared the same wall as a television and VCR perfect for recording and watching cooking shows.

The quiet hum of the refrigerator was barely louder than the air conditioner, and Betty smelled a faint, artificially freshened whiff of the litterbox she'd topped off with fresh litter that morning. Pearla's food dish and everything else was hidden away in the dishwasher and sparkling clean by now.

None of that was out of place or disturbed, and Betty was hard pressed to say what *did* catch her attention.

All she knew for certain was someone else had been inside since she'd stopped in long enough to collect Pearla before heading to Katie's.

She touched Travis's arm as he started to walk around her, heading for the sparkly red bowl on one of the dark gray granite countertops. The one piled high with whatever fruit was seasonal, or at least available at whatever grocery store one of them passed by.

Today that meant a bunch of bananas just getting

the perfect amount of brown spotting to make it clear they were ripe, along with oranges, tangerines, and grapefruits held over from winter. She knew from countless visits that Travis was about to grab a tangerine for himself and offer to peel one for her.

"Don't," she whispered. "Something's not right."

He turned, eyebrows raised in surprise.

Betty started to explain, but her voice died in her throat.

Now she understood the difference.

A blue and white label stood out on one of the bananas.

Not that unusual in any grocery store or most houses all over the country.

But one of Lee's odd quirks that Betty found far more endearing than strange concerned those stupid labels. Not that stores shouldn't have a way to keep track of fruit and get it scanned through the register and all. That wasn't the problem.

Lee despised the kinds of labels that were impossible to remove without tearing into the skin of the fruit, or else so flimsy that it took forever to scrape every last bit of them off. She couldn't say why. She'd just always hated them.

And so Betty followed Lee's longstanding habit of making sure to carefully remove them before the fruit hit the bowl.

Every single time. Including a couple of days ago.

Someone else had brought that bunch of bananas into the house.

And whoever killed Joey Wilkenson had used poison.

CHAPTER 25

Betty gripped Travis's arm and pulled him closer. His muscles fairly thrummed with tension.

"Someone's been here," she said almost against his ear. "Since this morning. Probably since I grabbed Pearla and went to Katie's, since I was able to get in and out, and she was fine."

Betty's gut clenched and her heart twisted at the thought of *any*one being in their house with Pearla. She rejected her brain's efforts to imagine what could have happened, since the intruder was quite possibly already a murderer.

She had to try twice to force enough air into her lungs to speak.

"We can't trust anything to eat or drink or who knows what the hell else in this house."

Travis let out a long breath, and his arm relaxed under Betty's hand.

"He might still be in here, Betty. Or close enough that he knows we're here. We've got to go. Now."

All at once, Betty understood what people meant by saying they saw red when fury overtook them. Her vision did darken, and all her senses seemed to compress and accelerate at the same time.

Every sparkle of light off the granite magnified to a spotlight in her eyes, and she would have sworn she could hear Travis's heartbeat along with her own. Her skin tingled with the faintest whisper of cool air stirring in the house as if she stood outdoors in a hurricane.

She wouldn't have believed it even five minutes ago, but now she smelled traces of soap in the dishwasher and the lingering remains of Lee's spicy perfume.

The trembling spreading through her body had nothing at all to do with fear.

Not any more.

It was the murderous asshole who'd invaded her home who needed to fear for his worthless fucking life.

This time her words came out in a fierce hiss.

"I'm not going *anywhere*. I spent enough time sneaking around and trying to avoid upsetting anyone for five lifetimes. He was a goddamn *idiot* for coming in here. If hc gets within my reach, he'll pay the price ten times over."

Before either of them could say another word, Betty's super-tuned hearing caught a whisper of movement from the other side of the kitchen.

She was sure it hadn't come from the bathroom

hidden away behind a heavy six-panel oak door, but from closer.

Maybe from the closet-sized pantry tucked behind a much thinner door.

She pointed toward it, not quite aware how hard she squeezed until Travis tried to slip his fingers under hers.

He shook his head, his voice low enough that she never would have heard it without her senses twisted into their highest possible gear.

"We *have* to call the police, Betty. If it's the same guy who came after Joey, all we know is he's crazy. He could have a knife or a gun in there."

Betty was amazed to have to fight back laughter.

Some part of her—long-ignored and assumed non-existent—was having the time of her life.

"He's a poisoner, remember? As long as he doesn't have some kind of spray or syringe at the ready, he doesn't stand a chance."

Travis shifted enough to get hold of Betty's shoulders, features far more twisted than his don't-go-there scowl. He spoke in a louder voice.

"Didn't you say you had a show about baking sourdough bread recorded? Maybe we could make some for Tasha since I keep hearing you complain about how your starter is getting out of control." He let go long enough to point toward the television, then whispered. "Go turn it on, so we can call the police. *Please*, Betty."

She was reasonably sure he knew Lee would never let their sourdough starter or anything else within her bread-baking reach get the least bit out of control, and entirely sure that wasn't the point.

Travis was as eager to distract her as to keep whoever was in the pantry from getting nervous and upset enough to act out.

What Betty wanted to do was grab one of her great-grandmother's big cast iron skillets from the rack over the stove, then throw the pantry door open and take her chances.

She might have done just that despite the desperate plea in his eyes.

Someone had invaded her *home!*

And it was pure dumb luck that Pearla hadn't been there alone when it happened.

But her eyes fell on a framed photo of herself and Lee on the same shelf as the cookbooks. They stood with their arms around each other, grinning at the camera through a mass of bright scarves and toboggans, in front of a huge snow-woman, complete with a long, blonde wig, bright red lips, and at least a G-cup's worth of snowy breasts.

Their trip to Wisconsin for Christmas three years ago.

Where Lee was right now, already worrying about Betty and Pearla getting too close to whoever had turned way too many people's lives upside down.

Then another shift from the pantry, this one loud enough that Travis looked that way too.

Through her anger, Betty was amazed anyone could

stand upright in there enough to close the door with random stacks of cans and jars along with a bag of cat food and a box of litter taking up only a few square feet of floorspace.

She took a deep breath and nodded.

She walked over and turned on the television, already set to a cooking channel. Instead of bread, the aggressively perky host was busily whipping up what looked like some kind of pie, but the commentary was loud and constant enough for their purposes.

"Fine. But I'm not going *anywhere*," she said, again close to Travis's ear. "Not until this asshole is out of here."

"Then you're stuck with me until that happens."

CHAPTER 26

TRAVIS MADE MORE noise than he needed to opening cabinets and closing them again, asking about baking pans and yeast, all while pointing toward the red phone on the wall under the cookbooks.

Betty clenched and unclenched her fists as she headed that way. She took the business card he held out, wondering if her hands would be shaking too hard to dial.

She managed it eventually, trying to convince herself that on one would answer or the detective would be out, and she and Travis would have to deal with the situation after all.

Only hoping a little that they'd get the chance.

"Detective Markov here."

"Betty Compton here," she said quietly. "Calling to let you know someone's switched out fruit in my house, and I think he's still here."

A beat of silence long enough that Travis asked where she kept the flour.

"Oh, that's in the pantry, Travis. Give me a second and I'll get it."

"Are you still *there*? I can have a car there in a few minutes, and myself in less than ten. Get the hell out, Betty!"

Something thudded against the pantry door loud enough to hear over the television and Travis's continued conversation with himself, and Betty jumped hard enough that she almost dropped the phone.

"I'm afraid we just ran out of time."

Betty put the phone down on purpose, ignoring Detective Markov's increasingly louder insistence that she and Travis needed to get out of the house.

Demanding that Betty to get out of *her own house*.

She stepped over to the stove and reached up for the biggest of her inherited cast iron skillets. Her great-grandmother had been gone for years, but Betty could almost see the cantankerous matriarch's approving smile and nod. And her own mother Charlene's mortified scowl.

Travis watched her settle the thick, reassuring handle into her fist with his mouth open.

Betty decided to give his fake train-of-talk one more push.

"Go ahead and grab the yeast out of the freezer, Travis, and I'll see what just fell over in the pantry."

But she pointed at the heavy marble rolling pin

sitting on its showy marble pedestal not far from the sink.

Neither she nor Lee much liked using it, since they both preferred the fun of drop-and-rip biscuits to fussier baking.

It still might turn out to be the most useful thoughtless gift her parents had ever given her.

Even better if the use was one that would have caused them both to clutch their pearls and gasp in horror.

She tried, but she couldn't quite hide her grin as she walked quietly toward the pantry.

At the idea of Walter and Charlene being shocked by her yet again, absolutely.

The deeper truth was her rising excitement at literally taking things into her own hands.

Not staying in the background hoping for someone else to solve the problem, or ignoring what happened, or pretending not to mind the trouble.

The door thudded again, and she noticed the little gap between the door and the floor was dark. Whoever was in there either was afraid to turn on the light or didn't know how.

Betty stopped on one side of the door, with Travis on the other, both of them wielding their culinary weapons.

It was time to get this settled one way or the other.

One more thud, and a low groan that cranked the exhilaration in her belly up another gear.

"Done enough damage in there?" Betty called in her sweetest voice. "Or do you want to trip and stumble a few more times while we wait for the police to get here? I expect you'll eventually figure it out if you don't manage to hit yourself on the head hard enough to knock yourself out first."

Travis nodded, his eyes bright with excitement—and more than a little fear.

"You're finished either way," he said. "It's just a question of how banged up you want to get before the police take you out of here."

The metallic clank of cans toppling over was followed by a muffled curse.

Betty decided to take a chance that might bring the whole frustrating situation to a close, at least as far as getting the drama the hell out of her house.

"Come on, Chris. It's over. Kicking around in my pantry isn't going to get you out of this mess."

Silence.

Long enough that Betty's arms ached from holding up the heavy skillet.

Travis started to reach for the pantry door's old brass knob, with Betty shaking her head at him. Visions of a cornered murderer throwing a can of peas hard enough to knock Travis out were too dangerous to be funny.

Then the doorknob squeaked as it turned.

And crashed open, nearly smacking Travis in the face.

Betty didn't see whether he blocked it or stepped out of the way.

She was too busy taking aim at the crouching figure trying to dart toward the back kitchen door.

At the last split second, she shifted from targeting the head and smashed toward the upper back instead.

The would-be-escapee sprawled full-length on the floor with a scream.

Travis immediately landed on top of the intruder's body, knees on either side of the waist, absurd marble rolling pin pressed on the back of the neck.

"Don't you fucking move," Travis growled, leaning close to a head full of sweaty blond hair. "Or one of us will crush your goddamn skull."

The man on the floor let out a long, low moan, rising to a frustrated howl.

But he was apparently smart enough to heed the warning to hold still.

CHAPTER 27

HE WORE ordinary black cargo pants and a brown t-shirt, and no watch or rings on his outstretched arms and hands. His face was turned away from her, but his ear, cheek, and neck were brick-red.

Betty knelt beside Travis, wincing at the stink of perspiration and...

The jackass had pissed himself when he hit the floor.

On her floor, in her house, on the tile Lee picked out.

She almost smacked him on the head with the skillet after all.

Would sharp-eyed Detective Markov believe self defense if it was obvious the guy had already been on the ground?

Would it be worth it even if the detective saw exactly what happened?

"What the *hell* were you doing in my pantry?" Betty said. "And who the hell are you?"

"I'll take my chances with the cops, you psychopaths!"

Travis looked at Betty, eyebrows raised.

"The person who broke into your house and hid in your pantry is calling us psychopaths. Isn't that fascinating? Think I should go ahead and see how hard I have to swing to shatter this rolling pin across the side of his head?"

"I think you just might have to. We did tell the police an intruder was in here. They'd understand if we had to defend ourselves. He clearly meant to hurt us."

The guy kicked his feet and clenched his fists.

"Hurt you how? Do you see a gun? A knife?"

Betty leaned over and tapped the skillet on the floor in front of his face. She wasn't quite proud of causing him to flinch away, but she didn't pretend to herself that she wasn't glad to see it.

"I'm going to take a guess that you know plenty about hurting people without a weapon. And I'm pretty sure my friend told you not to move. And I asked for your name. Are you trying to convince us you were randomly in my house for no reason at all, but you decided to hide when we got here anyway?"

She sat back and looked into Travis's blazing eyes.

"Wonder if he has any identification in all those pockets?" he said. "Maybe something like an Ohio drivers license?"

"Let me just take a look."

He once again tried to twist away, but Travis shifted right along with him.

Betty balancing her perfectly seasoned chunk of cast iron across the backs of his knees got him still in a hurry.

Thankfully she didn't have to get overly familiar to find what she was after. His wallet was buttoned into one of the side pockets of his cargo pants.

She flipped open the scuffed brown leather wallet and slipped a smudged license out.

She was hardly surprised by what she saw, but her stomach still clenched in sorrow and anger.

"Now I wonder why one Chris B. Mason, of Columbus, Ohio, found his way into my pantry? And what he might have had on his mind?"

Going by the way his jaw clenched and tears stood in his eyes, Travis struggled with the same twist of emotions.

He leaned forward, rapping a knuckle on the back of Chris's head.

"Care to elaborate on that, Chris? Because I'm kinda wondering what brought you all the way down here in the first place. Just a random vacation, maybe? Or a business trip? Could it be you took the chance to visit with dear friends you haven't seen for a while?"

Betty watched Chris's back rise as he drew in a big breath. She hoped she'd hit him hard enough with the skillet that breathing would hurt for a while.

Instead of the shout she expected, his voice was low and cold.

"Why I'm here is none of your damn business."

Betty moved until she sat cross-legged on the floor. She figured they only had a few minutes before Detective Markov arrived, and she wanted to make that time count.

Travis deserved to hear answers. Tasha did too, of course, but helping him was a start.

"I'd say it's very *much* my business," she said. "Since you're on my kitchen floor, and it sounds like you made a hell of a mess in the pantry. Want to try again? I've got several skillets where that one came from."

This time Travis leaned down and spoke almost into Chris's ear, sounding like the only reason he wasn't shouting was because his throat was too tight.

"Why did you go after Joey Wilkenson, Chris? What was worth coming to Atlanta and throwing the rest of your miserable life away?"

"Because he's the one who *made* my life miserable!" The volume was amazing with his face turned away and Travis perched not far from his lungs. "Got me and all my money roped into that business, then turned tail at the first sign of trouble and left me to try to pick up the pieces."

Travis shook his head and sat back, but he didn't move the heavy rolling pin away from Chris's neck.

"See, that's not what *I* heard at all. I heard you didn't even go in half on the business, not when it came to money. But when it started to take off, you were more than happy to drain everything you could back out. Took out a mortgage on the building without talking to Joey first, and acted like enough of an asshole that a bunch of your employees left at once. He carried you for a while, a *long* while, before he finally cut his losses and moved on."

Betty had read all of that in Joey's journal, but hearing Travis say it chilled her and infuriated her at the same time.

"And even if your version was true, Chris," she said, "that nowhere near justifies what happened to him. Georgia doesn't look too kindly on breaking and entering, but poisoners do a hell of a lot worse. Especially when those two crimes are related."

Chris's shoulders shook, and a low, unpleasant laugh oozed into the kitchen.

"I'm sure that would be a problem for someone who did all that. But all you got me on is being in the wrong place at the wrong time. Good luck trying to prove anything else."

CHAPTER 28

Betty got up to grab a paper towel, then used it to pick up the bunch of bananas out of the bowl on the counter. She heard a distant police siren, no doubt about to break up this disturbing little party.

She walked around to Chris's other side. What she could see of his face was blotchy and red.

"Maybe you're hungry after spending so much energy in the pantry. I'd be glad to give you something to eat. One thing about us Southerners and our hospitality is I'd hate to send you off to jail with an empty stomach."

She put the bananas on the floor less than an inch away from Chris's nose.

The way he drew back and struggled to move away even with Travis adjusting to every thrashing movement answered a hell of a lot of questions.

"Get those damn things away from me!"

Travis met Betty's gaze, and she knew both of them once again struggled with as much sadness as satisfaction.

What a terrible waste of Joey's life, and an attempted waste of Betty's and probably other people's as well.

"Just tell me why, Chris," Travis said, sounding as exhausted as Betty felt after the last few days. "Not about Joey, you've said enough about that until you talk to the police. But why go after Betty like this? And I can't imagine you weren't planning to target Tasha and me and probably others after that."

Chris stopped thrashing, but Betty could hear how hard he was breathing.

What she thought was a wheeze turned into a growl before he spoke.

"Because you all went along with it! What he did to me, you all thought it was reasonable to run someone into the ground then run away from the mess he made. I saw you at the fancy new building, then at Tasha's, then at some scum attorney's place. I wasn't about to pass up the good luck that led me. Right. *Here.*"

The flush on Betty's cheeks and throat had nothing to do with her hormones or even the weather for a change. Calling her sister a scum attorney flipped a switch in the middle of her brain that might not ever flip back.

She walked around and knelt she could see his face.

And so he could see her.

She waited until he rolled his one visible eye up into a pathetic glare.

"You're damn lucky the police are almost here. Because try as I might, I can't dig deep enough to find sympathy for you. Not when you felt perfectly justified to act as judge, jury, and executioner for Joey, and for people you didn't even know. This stunt could have killed my wife, or my sister, or one of her kids."

She used the paper towel to spin the bunch of bananas that neither she nor Lee had bought—and that she intended for Detective Markov to take out of there for analysis—in a slow circle in front of his nose.

He tried to draw back every time the bundled stems or splayed ends got near him.

"From the way you're acting, these might have even killed my cat if she'd gotten too close. Here's something to think about over the next several years of your miserable fucking life. If we hadn't accidentally stopped by here and caught you, and *any* of that had happened, you would have been a lot better off in prison than if I'd gotten my hands on you."

The sirens stopped outside the house, and Betty fought back an entirely unreasonable urge to laugh at the idea of their neighbors peeking around curtains to see what was going on. If she'd had any plans of trying to keep this Chris's appearance in the house secret from Lee, they'd just evaporated.

"Got anything else to ask him before the professionals take over?" she said.

Travis looked away from her for several seconds, and she wasn't surprised to see his chin quivering when he turned back.

"Just one thing that might not come up. I kinda doubt the police would notice an extra bruise on his head, say if this rolling pin happened to slip. What do you think, Betty?"

She nodded and smiled, now looking into Chris's frantically darting eye.

"I think you're right. After all, it's our word against his."

"What?" Chris whispered, before his voice rose toward a shout. "What the hell do you want from me? Haven't you done enough?"

Travis picked up the rolling pin, and for a few seconds, Betty was terrified he was really going to use it. Put every bit of his strength and anger and heartbreak into it and crush this murdering bastard's skull right there on her kitchen floor.

She might not blame him, but the idea was no less horrifying.

"You've done every bit of this to yourself, Chris," Travis said. "Now how about you tell me where I need to go to get Joey's Windy City mug back? I sure hope for your sake that you didn't do something stupid like throwing it away."

The one eye blinked, and Chris scowled.

"That nasty dented thing? *That's* what you're worried about?"

Travis shifted so Chris could see the heavy chunk of cold marble, the wooden handle touching the floor right beside the bananas.

"That's what I'm worried about. There's not much else left, is there? I guess the only question is how much you're worried about your head being intact when they haul you off to jail."

Betty barely had time to wonder if Travis hadn't just given Chris too much of an easy way out before Chris's back rose with an indrawn breath.

Instead of the scream or shout she'd been expecting, he only heaved a harsh sigh.

"Fine, you win. If you really want that cheap beat-up thing, it's at the hotel where I've been staying." His eye narrowed and a wicked grin twisted his mouth. "Been thinking about taking it home as a trophy to remember that asshole by. But I figure using it to put him in the ground will be sweet memory enough."

Someone pounded on the front door just as Travis's face contorted and went brick red.

"Police! Anyone inside?"

Betty grabbed Travis's arm before he could move, her heart twisting at how tense the muscles were even when he was shaking.

"We're inside!" she called. "The door is open!"

She shook her head and locked gazes with Travis.

"He's not worth it, and he never was. I think he knows that better than anybody. The real shame is Joey figured it out too late. Let the police take care of him. Then we'll take care of the rest."

CHAPTER 29

A FEW DAYS LATER, Betty had a hard time remembering how dreary and sad the East Lake Feline Emporium had seemed last time she was inside.

Right after she and Travis had almost managed to tempt Detective Markov into arresting them for Joey Wilkenson's murder. To be fair, they'd certainly asked for the extra scrutiny by showing up in the pre-dawn hours not long after the ransacking of Joey's office added insult to devastating injury.

Rather than scowling at Betty with eyes overflowing with suspicion, Detective Markov currently sat in one of the cat-fabric-cushioned chairs in the Emporium's waiting room, with an irresistible Pearla sitting in her lap.

Thankfully the detective had left her typical dark wardrobe behind, so the inevitable deposit of Pearla's long white hair blended with her faded jeans and gray t-shirt.

Katie's three feline kids roamed the subdued gathering as well, targeting the most cat-reluctant guests for personal attention. After getting to know each other during Betty and Pearla's stay, the four cats had advanced to the amused toleration of each other with occasional bursts of play stage.

Pretty much like a bunch of human cousins as far as Betty was concerned.

Katie leaned against the receptionist's desk chatting with Cortney, the young woman who finally had a clear prospect of keeping her new job now that the owner's murderer was firmly in custody. Unlike the other employees milling around, Cortney had been unable to resist wearing her uniform of a peach golf shirt sporting a gold-embroidered logo of three snuggly cats. The big change was she'd remembered her bright nametag on the opposite side.

That and her eyes were sad, but they'd lost the terrified and worried look from when she and Betty first met.

Katie'd left her believably conservative attorney-garb behind for this Saturday afternoon gathering, but she hadn't gone anywhere near as parent-proper as for her Easter party what seemed like a year ago. Her gauzy green dress might not look at home at the office, but Betty knew it suited her sister's personality a whole lot better.

This was hardly a party, but no one suffered the foul, barely drinkable coffee-like office sludge Betty and Travis had choked down, either. A variety of much better coffee, tea, and soda along with a hearty bunch of snacks from Tasha's overflowing house provided a far better alternative.

Getting some of the well-meaning but overwhelmingly generous offerings out of the house helped give Tasha the strength to attend this low-key re-opening, much like she'd faced the task of taking on both this and the dog-centered business without her husband by her side.

A gentle hand on her back let Betty know the most important attendee had discovered her almost-hidden perch beside a tall display full of luxurious cat beds that put most human furniture to shame. The most lovely, musical voice in the world spoke close to her ear.

"Thought you could put in an appearance and hide out from everyone at the same time? Did someone invite Charlene and Walter without telling me?"

Betty turned and got to her feet at the same time, stepping into Lee's warm and much-needed embrace. While her wife being away visiting family in Wisconsin had made a difficult week even tougher, every single hug since she'd gotten back evaporated a little more of the sorrow and stress.

"It's not quite as bad as a party with my parents," Betty said, brushing a wavy strand of Lee's lustrous black hair behind her ear. "But yeah, I don't mind staying a little bit out of the way for this one."

Green eyes that never seemed to miss any of Betty's attempts to hide her feelings searched for a long moment, then full, pink lips curved in a smile.

Even though she'd had to give up her much-loved flannel for springtime Atlanta, Lee still managed to look cool and breezy in a sunshine-yellow blouse. She took Betty's hand and kissed the back of it, sending tingles from Betty's head to her toes.

"Speaking of out of the way," Lee said, "when did you last see Travis?"

Betty frowned and scanned the group again.

"I see Nina talking to Tasha, but looks like he's disappeared. I've got a good idea where he is, though."

"Want company, or is this a solo comforting situation?"

Betty rolled her eyes in advance of the sappiness about to exit her own mouth, but unable to think of anything else to say.

"I *always* want your company, sweetheart. Whether you want to face the possibility of Travis in introvert mode is up to you."

Lee giggled and squeezed Betty's hand before she let go.

"Since I'm already in the midst of *Betty* in introvert mode, I believe I'll leave you to it. I'm overdue for a visit with Katie anyway." She kissed Betty's cheek before walking away.

Betty watched her go, wondering how quickly they could round up Pearla, escape, and get themselves back home.

But if she was right about where Travis had retreated to, he could likely use a sympathetic ear, from someone who actually *hadn't* known Joey, unlike just about everyone else.

Sometimes a bit of distance helped when it came to talking through grief.

Once she escaped to the darkened hallway beyond the reception area, Betty wasn't the least bit surprised to see Joey's office door open just enough to let light show through. She doubted anyone else would be back here, but she knocked anyway.

"Come on in," Travis called.

Betty couldn't quite work out what sounded odd about his voice until she opened the door.

Unlike the moody or at least melancholy expression she expected, Travis was smiling.

The far neater state of the office might explain some of that. All the odd knickknacks and collectibles were back on their shelves instead of thrown all over the floor. The desk itself held a phone and a huge calendar.

Betty's gaze went immediately to a dinged and scratched metal tankard beside the calendar, full of white-barreled ink pens rather than coffee or tea.

She couldn't read the whole thing, but *Windy City* was clearly visible.

Joey's missing mug, and apparently the murder

weapon. Detective Markov said Chris Mason had confessed to coating the inside of the mug with cyanide, then taking it with him after he returned to make sure it had been enough to kill Joey. A less-than-scrupulous locksmith had taught Chris how to let himself in and out, and now waited behind bars himself in connection with multiple crimes all over Atlanta.

That worse-for-wear mug was also the thing that'd kept Travis pushing until Joey's supposedly natural death was proven to be decided unnatural.

"What are you doing hiding back here?" she said.

Travis shook his head, but he was still smiling. He held up his own little gray Nokia phone.

"You're about as likely to believe me as Detective Markov was last time we were here."

"I've known you a lot longer than she has, so I'm immune to your usual line of nonsense. Try me."

He put the phone on Joey's desk—now Tasha's desk unless she eventually hired another manager for the cat side of the business—and spun it like a top.

"Well, I just had a rather unexpected phone call from Walter."

Betty tried to stop it, but her jaw dropped.

"Walter as in my father? Husband of Mrs. Charlene McHale Compton? Please tell me he wasn't an asshole to you."

Travis shook his head slowly and set the Nokia to spinning again.

"Far from it. He called, my dear Betty, to *thank* me. Apparently he and Charlene have decided that if I hadn't been with you at your house the other day, some sort of dire fate would have befallen you. Walter actually said, and I quote, 'Our Betty's lucky you were there, and lucky to have you as a good friend.'"

Betty snorted out laughter.

"*Bull*shit. All Walter could talk about after Katie let it slip what happened—and I still haven't figured out how she'll have to make up for that one—was how Lee and Pearla and I needed to stay somewhere else until pretty much everything in the house was taken out and destroyed. He couldn't hear me no matter how many times I told him that the police had cleared out the likely food and given the all-clear."

Travis nodded, still smiling.

"Oh, don't worry, he and Charlene still prefer you all vacate the premises for a while. At a hotel, of course. There was no mention of staying at their house, mind you. But he most certainly did thank me. I'm glad I was back here, because anyone witnessing me trying to force enough air into my lungs to squeak out a thank you would have been rolling on the floor laughing."

"Well I'll be damned," Betty said, finally smiling herself. "Who knew the old man had it in him? Good for you, Trav."

He waved a hand toward her.

"That was a nice enough start for me, but what he

and Charlene really need to do is get those sticks out of their asses long enough to realize how grateful they should be to know *you*, too. Since he managed that much with me, maybe he'll eventually work the rest out."

It was Betty's turn to blush. But she couldn't quite bring herself to argue the point.

"Thank you for telling me, either way. Listen, are you doing all right? Being back here and all?"

This time his smile was sad.

"I'm all right. Not great, but better. Just having the police take it seriously helped a lot, and having that monster behind bars helps a lot more. The rest will take time. I just wish he was still here."

Betty crossed the room and hugged Travis from behind.

"Joey was damn lucky to have you as a good friend. And Walter's right that I am too."

Travis squeezed her arms and got to his feet.

"I'm guessing someone sent you back here to fetch me?"

"Not quite. Lee was just wondering where you were."

Travis joined Betty at the door, then looked back toward the desk.

"Thanks for putting up with me lately, Betty. I still wish you'd had a chance to get to know him. And I know his murder never would have been solved without Katie. And even more, without you."

Betty linked her arm through his as they headed down the hall.

"Thank you. I say we should encourage Walter and Charlene in their beliefs. But I suspect both of us will feel a lot better once we make sure most of the credit goes to Pearla where it truly belongs."

ABOUT KARI

Kari Kilgore's wanderlust and imagination lead her all over the world on grand adventures. Her heart and family bring her home to her native Appalachian Mountains of Virginia. From that solid base and with the help of the ever-changing lens of her imagination, she brings those adventures to life in fiction.

While her cats are indeed fabulous and she was a pet groomer in a past life, thankfully the murderous sort of drama remains firmly on the page.

Kari writes mystery, contemporary fiction, fantasy, science fiction, and romance, and she's happiest when she surprises herself. She lives with her husband Jason A. Adams, various house critters, and wildlife they're better off not knowing more about.

The Confidential Adventure Club

For Kari's exclusive free After The End stories and deleted scenes, discounts, early pre-sale releases, adorable pet photos, and a whole lot more not available anywhere else, join us in The Club.

Hope to see you there!

www.KariKilgore.com
www.SpiralPublishing.net
www.ConfidentialAdventureClub.com

BB bookbub.com/authors/kari-kilgore

a amazon.com/author/karikilgore

g goodreads.com/karikilgore

f facebook.com/kari.kilgore.1

ALSO BY KARI KILGORE

I hope you enjoyed reading *Murder at the Fabulous Feline Emporium* as much as I enjoyed writing it.

For more stories featuring our furry feline friends, with more on the way, take a peek at www.KariKilgore.com/Cats.

To dive into more stories of mystery and crime, investigate www.KariKilgore.com/Mystery. For more tales with LGBTQ+ characters in almost every genre, head over to www.KariKilgore.com/LGBTQStories.

For more novels, novellas, and short stories where speculative elements are either slight or not there at all, pay a visit to to www.KariKilgore.com/ContemporaryFiction.

Be the first to know about release dates and check out more of my fiction, including almost every genre, at www.KariKilgore.com.

The Storms of Future Past Series:

Dreaming the Storm

Joining the Storm

Into the Storm

Fighting the Storm

Storms of the Heart: A Storms of Future Past Romance

Storms of Future Past Books One through Four Collection

The Odd Society:

Independent by Means of Magic

Protected by Means of Magic

The Voices through Time Series:

Songs in the Mountain

Secrets in the Land

Sorrows in the Earth

Walking the Ghosts: A Voices through Time Novella

Dispatches from the Galaxy Stories:

Restricted Species

The Becalmed

The Garbage Belt

Plurapod Pathogen

The Changes Cascade

Novels:

Until Death

The Dream Thief

Hand Me Downs

Protecting Her Own

The Coffee Bomb and the Corporate Spy

The Great Gold Record Heist

Novellas:

Legacy of the Land

In the Pines

DNA Never Lies

The Box of Possibilities

Collections and Anthologies:

Fantastic Women: A Dark Fantasy Novella Trio

Fantastic Shorts: Volume 1

Near Future Forward (with Jason A. Adams)

Fantastic Shorts: Volume 2

Partners in Romance (with Jason A. Adams)

Dispatches from the Galaxy: A Space Opera Novella Trio

Fantastic Shorts: Volume 3

Escape into Romance: A Collection of Sweet Beginnings

Stepping Out of Reality: Short Spells of Appalachian Magic

Facing Down Extraordinary: A Series of Ordinary Heroes

Hacking Cybercrime: Dana Sanderson Short Mysteries

Shadows Mountain Deep (with Jason A. Adams)

Investigations Beyond Belief: The Initial Adventures of Deb Powers: Otherworldly PI

Passages in the Real World: Six Stories of Life's Transitions

Fantastic Side Trips: Side Characters Take Center Stage

A Kaleidoscope of Cat Tales: Five Stories of Cats and People Who Love Them

A Tapestry of Holiday Tales: Winter Adventures from the Odds and Endings Bookstore

Uncommon Holidays: A Different Side of the Season (with Jason A. Adams)

Aunties Among Us: Five Tales of Fabulous Women

Four-Legged Heroes: When Pets Rescue People

Partnership in Crime: Six Journeys to Justice (with Jason A. Adams)

www.ingramcontent.com/pod-product-compliance
Lightning Source LLC
Chambersburg PA
CBHW050332110726
47899CB00007B/2473